THE
ICARUS
SHOW

www.**davidficklingbooks**.com

The Icarus Show
is a
DAVID FICKLING BOOK

First published in Great Britain in 2016 by
David Fickling Books,
31 Beaumont Street,
Oxford, OX1 2NP

Text © Sally Christie, 2016

978-1-910200-48-3

1 3 5 7 9 10 8 6 4 2

David Fickling Books supports the Forest Stewardship Council (FSC), the
leading international forest certification organisation. All our titles that are
printed on Greenpeace-approved FSC-certified paper carry the FSC logo.

DAVID FICKLING BOOKS Reg. No. 8340307

A CIP catalogue record for this book is available from the British Library

Printed and bound in Great Britain by Clays Ltd, St Ives plc

THE ICARUS SHOW

SALLY CHRISTIE

David Fickling Books

31 Beaumont Street
Oxford OX1 2NP, UK

CHAPTER 1

COMING SOON

I was on the school bus, going home, when I found it. I opened my bag to get out my book, and spotted it straight away. Someone had put it there, tucked it inside the secret pocket where I keep my spare pen and my money for lunch. There'd been 20p change that day. As I searched for my book, I did a quick check: still there. My fingers touched *it* as they felt for the coin.

All the way home I kept my book open and turned a page now and then. But I wasn't really reading. I was congratulating myself on my outstanding self-control. Don't React. That was my new Lambourn motto. Don't miss a beat.

I'd got the idea from Shadow, I think, who was

definitely the expert. If you put Shadow outside when she'd been on the sofa, she never tried to run back in. She'd just sit down and wash herself, then saunter away. She made you believe it was what she'd always wanted.

The opposite was what David Marsh had done on the first day of term. Alan Tydman had stuck out a foot to trip him up. He did it to everyone – but David Marsh had turned round and come back. Come right back to Alan and said, 'Was that you?' Big mistake. Now we all called him David Bog and he must have wished he'd just laughed and carried on, like a normal person.

I am a normal person. No one will ever change *my* name. I'm constantly on my guard to protect my status. It's hard work because you can be put to the test any time: scooped up and shoved out into the garden if you're a cat; tripped up and shoved in the ribs by Alan Tydman if you're a person in our year at Lambourn Secondary School.

Or have a sealed brown envelope put in your bag.

Don't React. Don't miss a beat.

When the bus reached my stop, I closed my book. No

one would notice my bookmark hadn't moved because no one was sitting beside me. Good. But Bogsy was already getting off. Bad. If he got off first, I had to hang back to make sure I didn't get off *with* him – since it was only us two at this stop. Once, I had waited too long and missed my chance to get off altogether. Everybody had laughed and I'd nearly panicked. But then I'd laughed, too, at myself – made a funny, 'Stupid Me' face and saved the situation. I'd had to get off at the next stop, and walk an extra kilometre home, but that didn't matter.

Today I just had to dawdle a bit to put distance between Bogsy and me. I got home safely, and went straight down the garden to Don's shed.

You need to understand about Don's shed. It's important, so I'll tell you: it's not really Don's shed, it's ours. Don's dead. He was old and he died and Maisie went into a Home. There. Now you know. Even though Maisie and Don had been our next-door neighbours – the houses are joined – we sold ours and bought theirs and moved in. We did it because of their garden, which is bigger than our old one. Mum and Dad fancied growing their own vegetables, just like Don.

Anyway, Don's shed is nice. It's old and it's full of Don's stuff, which I like. Mum and Dad's stuff still stands in one corner, as if it's dropped by but hasn't been asked to sit down.

I sat down now – on an old wooden box – and opened my bag.

The strange thing about the envelope was it didn't have my name on. It didn't have anyone's name on. It was blank. Envelopes from teachers say, 'To the parents of Alex Meadows' – and anyway you get given them, they don't just turn up in your bag. Invitations to people's parties get put in your bag – Timmy still gets them – but people don't have that kind of party in my year any more. I think they go to the cinema with just one or two good friends. I'm not really sure.

Anyway, this envelope was mysterious – sinister, even. I was glad I'd handled the situation so well and was able to open it alone. I unsealed the flap and took out a slip of paper. A feather came out of the envelope, too, and fell to the floor.

Those were the only two things. The feather was grey and looked like a pigeon's. The paper was white, with computer writing on. But the writing didn't make sense. 'Coming soon!' it said. 'A boy is going to fly! Do you believe it? Can you believe it?? Will you be there???'

I quickly glanced up at the cobwebby window of Don's shed. Autumn sunshine filtered through dust. A largish spider in one corner. But nobody watching. No one (not counting the spider) there.

In a way, it *was* like an invitation. Invitations used to end with things like, 'Hope to see you there!' But invitations said where 'there' was – and also when – and who was asking. There was so much missing from this – it made me nervous. Somebody had a plan and I was in it but they weren't giving out the details and so I was at a disadvantage.

And what kind of plan was it, anyway? Crazy! A boy is going to fly? How? Like a bird? That's what the feather suggested, but that was mad. Or was this boy going to fly in a plane? Go on a holiday and I was to see him off? That made hardly more sense than the bird. What was the big deal in that? There seemed no explanation between the boring and the totally unbelievable.

But maybe unbelievable was the point. I was being dared to believe. Someone was challenging me to react, watching to see what I'd do. I looked again towards the window. This time I noticed a fly had been caught at one edge of the spider's web. The spider was spidering over to take a look. Maybe finish it off.

I felt horribly trapped. This whole thing was a trap. Did I believe that a boy was going to fly? What if I did? Would somebody laugh? And what if I didn't? Didn't – or couldn't. Would somebody call me useless?

My stomach felt so tight, it ached. Flying boys: I didn't want to know. But here was this envelope, forcing the question. Could I believe it? Would I believe it? I squirmed on my seat. Was I *supposed* to believe it?

Well, was I? What was the right thing to do?

CHAPTER 2
MAISIE

Looking back on what happened, I have an idea that life's like a fruit machine. That's a simile. You get marks for those, only Mr Smith says they're like chocolate éclairs: however good they are, it *is* possible to have too many.

What I mean by the fruit machine is that life's full of zillions of different combinations of things, some good, some bad, all spinning round all the time. And you think you can control which combination you end up with, but you can't. If I could have pulled a lever in Year 6 to keep things as they were, I would have: Maisie and Don our next-door neighbours; me in top year of primary school, with a really great best friend as well, and a cat. That would certainly count as a line of cherries in the fruit machine display, but could I hold on to it? All I've got left from that line-up is Shadow.

Actually, maybe there's one other thing. Maybe. But I'd better not include it because you shouldn't count your chickens before they've hatched. That's a cliché, and Mr Smith says *they're* always bad.

The day I heard Phil was moving away, I ran round to Maisie and Don's. Maisie was in the kitchen, making strawberry jam in her huge copper pan. As soon as I came in, she splopped some jam into a saucer for me to dip my finger in. But not for the reason you'd think. (That was Maisie all over.)

'Tell me,' she said, 'does that wrinkle when you push it?'

'Maisie,' I said, 'I've got terrible news! Phil's family are moving!'

'Sh!' she said. 'Don's asleep in the front room, having his after-lunch nap.'

'Phil's family are moving!' I said again, this time in a whisper.

'Phil? Your – friend?' said Maisie. 'Oh. Now, have you

tested that drop in the saucer? Push your finger through and tell me what happens.'

What happened was the path my finger made through the jam was immediately covered over again as if it had never been there.

'Nothing happens,' I said. 'It's too runny. It just flows back. Phil –'

'Then it's not nearly ready,' she said, and went on stirring.

There was a pause. The jam smelt delicious. 'D'you need this bit, for the saucepan?' I ventured. 'Or could I . . . ?'

She looked so angry, I thought I'd been wrong to drop the hint.

But, 'Saucepan?' she burst out. 'Saucepan? This was my mother's *preserving* pan! Now.'

She always said *Now* like that when she'd dealt with a subject once and for all. There was nothing more to be said about her mum's pan – but I cautiously sucked my finger. When I looked up, she was watching me.

'Nice?' she said.

'Mm.'

You see, I knew Maisie so well. People even assumed she was my gran. For instance, Phil did. The first time he came round my house, I took him over to Maisie and Don's, to meet them, and afterwards he asked me, 'Why do you call them Maisie and Don? It's weird.'

'It isn't,' I said, surprised. 'Maisie and Don are their names.'

'I mean,' said Phil, 'why not call them Gran and Grandad, or Granny and Grandpa?'

When I explained that they weren't my grand-parents, just neighbours I'd had all my life, he seemed to relax.

'I don't like her – Maisie,' he said. 'And I don't like that thing round her neck.'

I wasn't surprised by either statement. The 'thing round her neck' was a necklace, which I'll talk about later. And Maisie herself, it was true, had been *very* abrupt with him, even for her. I knew she didn't like him (so the feeling was mutual) but I didn't know why. I didn't tell Phil, of course, but I never took him back there. All Maisie knew from then on was what I told her: the things we got up to at school.

'Phil,' she said now, as she stirred the jam. 'Wasn't it Phil who dared you to wee on the classroom floor?'

It was. Phil always livened things up. He was great.

'And when you did, wasn't it Phil who went and told the teacher?'

'Yes, but that was ages ago, back in Year 1 or Year 2. He wouldn't do that now . . .'

'*I should hope not!*' said Maisie.

'Anyway, what does it matter?' I remembered my upset. 'He's moving to Scotland. I may never see him again!'

And Maisie said, 'Well, there are plenty more fish in the sea.'

I knew she didn't like him. I shouldn't have expected sympathy from her. But she needn't have made it *so* obvious. I felt offended.

'That's a cliché,' I said rudely (not caring if she knew the word or not).

'It's a fact,' she said. '*Now.*' (And I never found out if she did.)

Maisie's theory was that secondary school would be a fresh start. I'd meet loads of new people, she said, and sooner or later I'd find someone on my wavelength (her words).

'Somebody good enough. Somebody you can rely on.'

Apart from what this implied about Phil, it implied that at secondary school I'd be able to pick up where I'd left off. I'd find a new best friend and carry on just as before, as if nothing had happened. Everything would be the same. Only better.

But it wasn't.

Bad things happened that summer. Hardly had the jam cooled in its jars, than Don died. And after that, Maisie went funny. Not that you'd know, to talk to her, but apparently she could no longer go on living safely at home. Almost at once, she went into a Home, which sounds similar but is completely different. For a start, you can't make jam in a Home. Maisie had loved making jam – and chutney – and talking to people in her kitchen, as she peeled the potatoes.

People like me.

So, when I started at Lambourn Secondary, everything had changed. And I hadn't been there a week before I realized *I'd* better change, too.

If you opened a door when Shadow was walking past, she'd just keep walking. She was great. You knew she knew the door was open and that (being a cat) she really wanted to go through. She would in the end, if you left it open, but at least to begin with she'd done that thing of choosing not to.

It was Friday when I'd brought the terrible envelope home from school. For the rest of the day I did nothing, told no one, about it. I could have shown it to Mum or Dad, or Timmy, but I didn't. Trust No One. That was another new saying of mine.

Not that I couldn't trust my family. Well, I couldn't entirely trust Timmy. But Timmy couldn't have written the note because it had come from school. Besides, he doesn't use the spellcheck and he'd never have got the 'i' and the 'e' the right way round in 'believe'.

But by the next day, I had to tell someone. Before, I'd have gone round to Maisie and Don. And – well, I know it sounds funny, but I had discovered I still (half) could. I'd taken to getting the bus into town every Saturday morning, you see, to visit Maisie in The Laurels. And it was no ordinary visit. Talking to Maisie in The Laurels was like stepping into a different world.

The thing was, Maisie had managed to do what I'd failed to do in Year 6. She'd pulled the lever of the fruit machine and got a line of cherries! She'd engineered herself a world that, in many ways, seemed normal, but was actually not the same as everyone else's. For example, on Planet Maisie, Don was alive.

And so she lived happily there, and for an hour every Saturday morning – so did I. Now I was at Lambourn, any escape from the real world was good.

Maisie and I would talk about home, and what was growing in the garden. Maisie had good ideas about things and was still as decided as ever in her opinions. She would ask how the apples were doing – or the beans – or potatoes – and if Shadow was keeping down the mice.

I was careful *not* to ask how much she knew beyond that: where she thought she was now – and why – and what had happened. Someone less tactful might have asked, but not me. I stuck to neutral questions or asked her advice about history homework. Today, of course, I could hardly wait to tell her about the mysterious note, but I thought I should work around to it gently. So, once she had shut the door of her room and turned the TV off and got me a biscuit, I just said ever so casually, 'Can you read?'

It was a miscalculation.

'*Can I read?*' she exploded. 'I'm not *that* old! I didn't spend my childhood selling matches! I went to school and learned things, same as you! Now.'

'Sorry,' I said, 'it's just that you seem to like TV.'

'And how do I know what's on, eh? Had you thought of that?'

I didn't say, but it seemed to me that what was on didn't really matter to Maisie. Since she'd come to The Laurels, the TV was pumping stuff out pretty much all the time; she watched whatever. But, 'You read the listings?' I said, which was the right answer because she said, 'Hmph,' and gave me a stare.

'I've had a note from school,' I went on.

'In trouble, are you?' she said.

'No. Well, maybe. But it's not a note from a teacher. I don't know who it's from.'

I got it out, now a bit scrumpled, and she asked me to hand it over. 'Pass me my specs, too, will you?' Another hard stare. 'My *reading* glasses.'

She studied the note.

'Anonymous, eh?'

I knew what anonymous meant, but was ever so slightly surprised that she did. To hide my surprise, I said quickly, 'I think it's some kind of invitation.'

'I don't,' said Maisie. 'Invitations are personal. This hasn't got your name on. Did it come in an envelope? Did that have your name on?'

'No. Yes. I mean, it did come in an envelope, but the envelope was –' I wanted another word like her 'anonymous', but different, to show I was keeping up. 'The envelope was – impersonal,' I finished. 'You know, blank.'

I hurried on. 'But I know it was meant for me because somebody put it in my bag.'

'*I* think it's an advert,' said Maisie. 'Coming soon! That sounds like a show. Did all your friends get one as well?'

'I don't know. I only found it when I got home from school yesterday,' I lied. 'I haven't had a chance to talk with the others.'

'Well, what about him next door? The one who moved in?'

'He's not my friend.'

Did I mention that when we bought Maisie and Don's house, the Marshes bought ours? It was really unlucky. They had nothing to do with us and were completely new to the area; they could have chosen *anyone's* house. The fact they chose ours meant I had to work extra hard to have nothing to do with Bogsy.

Maisie looked at me sharply, then looked away. 'That's a pity,' she said. She fingered her necklace.

She always wore her necklace, a disc on a chain. The chain was thin, but must have been strong, since the disc was quite big. When Maisie folded her fingers around it, she could only just enclose it in her hand.

When I was little, I'd wanted to touch it, enclose it in mine. Its surface was heaped with yellowy-white things and fragments of shiny metal all bound together in a circular pattern by layers of black thread. It was intricate and unusual: far too fine to be factory-made.

'I like your necklace,' I'd said one day, and she'd jumped down my throat.

'My *pendant*, you mean!'

I'd asked her what it was made of and reached out to touch it but she'd drawn back.

'Rats' teeth and razor blades! Not for the likes of you.'

I had no reason not to believe her, though what she had said was so strange. The metal bits could have been anything and the white things could have been grains of rice, but I did believe her, unquestioningly. I still do.

I knew I had sounded childish when I'd said Bogsy wasn't my friend. 'Well, anyway,' I said. I felt caught out and I snatched the note back. 'Well, anyway, it can't be an advert. It doesn't say what you need to know. How can you "be there" if there's no address?'

'Haven't you heard of a teaser campaign?' said Maisie. I hadn't. 'Yes, but . . . It's all stupid!' I blustered.

'This is to get you interested,' she went on. 'To get you wondering, whet your appetite. Then there'll be something else, to whet it some more, before . . . all is revealed! How exciting!'

I needed to bring her back to the problem. 'So, is this boy going to fly, or isn't he?'

'*Course* not!' she snorted. 'Boys don't fly any more than pigs. Not in the normal run, anyway. But something is going to happen, and soon. That's all we can say at this stage.'

'Oh!' I broke in. 'I forgot! There was something else in the envelope. A feather.' I hadn't brought it with me, but the news stopped Maisie in her tracks.

'A feather? Now that is interesting. You know, in the First World War, they used to send feathers to the conshies. White ones. Conscientious objectors, you know, the ones who didn't want to fight because they thought it was

19

wrong. People sent them feathers to taunt them, to say they were cowards, just pretending.' She paused. 'I dare say some of them were.'

'Was Don a conshie? A real one?' I asked.

'*Don?*'

'I just thought maybe he didn't go along with the war . . .' I said that because it seemed to me he'd always stood for peace. Maisie liked to express opinions and I don't mean that he never did, but he'd always prefer to agree than to fight.

'You want to think a bit straighter, you do. Don wasn't even *born* then! Nother biscuit?'

'No, thanks,' I said. I glanced at the clock on the wall. 'I've got to go.'

As I put my coat back on, she softened and asked about the garden.

'Tell him not to pick the tomatoes,' she said and I knew who she meant. 'He always wants to pick them too soon, then it's chutney, chutney, chutney. There's not a hint of frost in the air – still plenty of ripening time. Tell him.'

It was funny, in one way she certainly was what Dad

called 'confused'. Confused about Don. But she wasn't one bit confused on the subject of green tomato chutney.

'I'll tell him,' I promised – and felt that I would, and even heard Don's reply, in my head: 'Right you are! She's the boss!'

Perhaps I was no less confused than her.

As I sat on the B17 going home, I thought how weird the world was – not just Maisie's, but this so-called normal world, too – in so many ways. Maybe pigs might fly, after all.

Maybe even a boy.

CHAPTER 3
WHO ELSE?

I didn't think Maisie was right about the feather. The one in the envelope had been grey, not white. Besides, as the message had been about flying, it was far more likely to be connected with that than with me not doing something, me being a coward.

But she did have a point about who else had got an envelope. That was important to find out. If a load of the others had got one, too, that would make the whole thing into some sort of advertising campaign, like she said. If I was the only recipient, that would be personal.

Of course, I really hoped it would turn out to be the loads-of-other-people option. The problem was how to find out.

Then on Monday morning, at the bus stop, I had a piece of luck. There was me, standing at one end of the shelter; there was Bogsy, at the other. The shelter smelt of wee, but because of the things people said at school, I had begun to believe it was him. I really had.

Anyway, suddenly, drifting about between us, was a feather.

It was just like the one in my envelope, so – although I'd left mine in Don's shed – for a moment I had this urge to go and pick it up. Then I remembered, Don't React – and a split second later, Don't worry, it's not even mine. But Bogsy was moving forward to get it. *It was his.*

Bogsy had got one, too! It wasn't just me, then! It couldn't be personal. I was so relieved, for a moment I didn't think any further than that. Bogsy stretched out his hand to grab the feather, and when it skittered away, he jumped on it heavily, with both feet. Then he shoved it in his bag.

So much for not reacting, I thought. I felt deeply contemptuous of him. So much for keeping things safe in the first place. He was useless. I was superior. Wait till I told them on the bus!

And that's when the horrible doubt crept in. What if I got on the bus and went straight to the back, where Alan Tydman sat, and said, 'Hey, Al, you know these feathers? Bogsy just dropped his! He nearly lost it! I saw! He can't even handle a little thing like that!'

And what if Alan Tydman said, 'What feathers?'

The thing was, it *could* still be personal. It could be personal to me and Bogsy, which would be worse. Somebody could be singling us out – saying, You're two of a kind.

Birds of a feather!

Whoever it was could be making the point, You *both* smell.

So when I got on the bus, I said nothing. I went to the back, but had to sit down before I reached Alan. The closest I could get was a seat next to Jack, a good mate of his. Jack Tweedy, who helped with his business and was – not counting Rob Bone, who was closest of all – his second in command.

'Hey,' I said briefly.

And Jack said, 'All right.'

Then we both looked away. I wouldn't have expected more, that was normal.

Only *something* was wrong. It wasn't just Jack and me who weren't talking: nobody was.

Had they all fallen silent when Bogsy and I got on, or had they been silent before? Usually the bus was so noisy, you had to shout to make yourself heard. Were they all in this together? Watching, waiting to see what we'd do? I looked cautiously sideways at Jack – and caught him looking sideways at me! In a panic, I looked across the aisle, to where Tom Flynn and Damien Crawley were sitting. Tom was absorbed in picking his nose, but Damien, like Jack Tweedy, *was* watching – secretly, out of the corner of his eye. Not me, though: Tom!

Was everyone watching each other? Weird! What for? And why the feathers? Was it just Bogsy and me who'd received them? If so, we were caught in a trap, for sure. Everyone else was watching for the secret sign to pounce.

It seemed unfair. I'd worked so hard to avoid this kind of thing. There was nothing I could do now, though, but watch and wait. It's odd how you end up acting the same, no matter if you're a spider or a fly.

Alan's little white bags were going much more slowly than usual today. The first coin to come up the aisle wasn't till we'd reached the start of the bypass. I took it from Hannah Dunbar, who said, 'Andy P', and I passed it on. I hardly had to repeat the name – since the bus was so quiet, everyone would have heard it first off. But I knew how important it was for Alan to have the details of each of the orders correct. Sometimes he made adjustments to the contents of a bag, according to who his customer was and how he was feeling towards them that day. When Andy P's bag came back down the aisle, it was floppy: almost empty. Poor Andy P.

Alan bought sweets at the Cash and Carry and bagged them up and sold them. Some days he sold so much on the bus, there was nothing left by break. But today there'd be plenty. I'd only had to pass two little bags back to Hannah by the time we reached school.

In our form room, waiting for Miss McGowan, things were slightly better. Not because Alan's gang were being any different to how they'd been on the bus – but because Lydia and Candy and their lot were in the mix now, and they were the opposite. Lydia and Candy never stopped chatting – and they didn't today. They didn't seem to notice the tension, they just went on and on and on – as usual, about boys. Nobody normally listened to them, but now, because no one else was talking, they were harder to ignore. *Tee hee, giggle giggle.* It got on your nerves. *Will he or won't he? Do you or don't you?* They seemed to be on about one boy in particular all the time; I didn't catch who. Even though it was good that the silence was over, it still wasn't great with them going on. Candy's voice was especially annoying, high pitched and shrill, rising now and then to a screech. 'Well, I don't!' she piped up now, over Lydia. 'I don't believe in fairies *or* Father Christmas – and *nobody's* going to fly!'

Well!

When she said that, it was like someone dropping a match in a can of petrol.

WHUMP! The room exploded. People were shouting, jumping up, racing round, grabbing bags, getting things out of them, upsetting chairs. Slips of paper came out – and feathers! Loads of feathers.

Alan was shouting, 'Shut up!' and everyone else was on about flying. Was someone going to, and when, where and why? I wanted to laugh. I did laugh! Alan had a feather – same as mine, same as Bogsy's. He held it up, scanning the room for the culprit, for the one who had dared to insult him like this. 'Who's the joker?' he roared. 'Who's been messing about?' Although there was still lots of noise in the room, he was slowly but surely regaining control.

I couldn't understand why he hadn't held his feather up before. Someone in my position had to be careful – trust no one – but Alan? Alan Tydman, who had a gang? People even called it Alan's Battalion because he was going to join the army when he left school. Someone like that wouldn't need to be careful, would they? So why hadn't he said something on the bus?

Anyway, now he was looking around to see who the

joker was. Candy said, 'Yeah, come on!' and there was more shouting.

Alan started picking on anyone he suspected of hanging back. He asked Peter Horn, who had a stammer, if he'd got anything to say. Peter said, 'N-n-n-n-' and Alan moved on.

'Meadows!' he barked at me. 'You get a note?'

'Yeah!' I said. 'In my bag. Friday.'

'Where is it now?'

'I – er – somewhere . . . At home.' Of course, I had hidden it in Don's shed, but I wasn't going to say that. My hesitation looked bad and I wondered if Alan was going to notice. He didn't. He was looking round again.

'Bogsy! Oi, Stinking Bog! What about you?'

Bogsy looked Alan straight in the eye and *he only went and did it again!* Like the time Alan tripped him up and he came back to face him. This time, instead of answering, he said – nothing. I ask you, how *stupid*. He wasn't so much an objector as a conscientious idiot.

Alan looked angry and I saw my chance.

'Yes, Al. He's got one. A feather. I saw it this morning. He dropped it. He can't even handle . . .'

Alan Tydman was someone who made you do things you knew you shouldn't. I don't mean like Phil, when he dared me to wee on the floor. With Alan, you didn't do things for fun; you did them because he had leadership qualities. He was an organizer and it's good to be organized. But I wouldn't have wanted Maisie to know I'd grassed someone up, even Bogsy. Even over a feather. I could guess what she'd say. I wouldn't have been proud of *myself* if I'd taken the time to think it through.

But that was the Alan Tydman effect. You *didn't* think. If Alan had told me to kick Peter Horn because of his stammer . . . Well, luckily, he didn't.

And luckily, almost at once Miss McGowan came in and called for quiet and the boring stuff of the day began.

When I walked in through the front door that evening, I thought I'd made a mistake with Alan. I could have showed him the feather after all. It had been in my bag all along. Funny, I thought I'd put it under a plant pot in

Don's shed. But here it was, slipped down between my books: my fingers felt it. They closed on it. Pulled it out.

And then I saw that I hadn't made a mistake. This feather was different. Grey, like the first, if perhaps slightly darker, but with something sellotaped on to the quill. A bit of paper – a tag. And on it was writing, computer writing. The writing said, 'ICARUS'.

CHAPTER 4
ICARUS

Mr Smith was a joker. He was our English teacher. The first day we had him, he got us to practise pronunciation by making us all sing this ridiculous song about eating apples and bananas. 'I like to eat – eat, eat, eat – apples and bananas,' and, 'I like to oot – oot, oot, oot – ooples and banoonoos.' It was completely stupid, they wouldn't even sing it in Timmy's class, I doubt, but by the time we'd got through all the different sounds – with Mr Smith deliberately getting them wrong half the time – we were in stitches.

Now we were on Greek myths, which Mr Smith really seemed to like. When he told us about Odysseus escaping from the Cyclops by clinging on under a sheep, he lay on his back underneath a table and hooked his arms and legs round the edges so he could actually hoist himself up off the floor for a few seconds. When he couldn't hang on any longer, he plopped back down and went, 'BAA!' really loudly. We fell about.

Already in English, nothing would have surprised us. We wouldn't have put anything past Mr Smith. I exchanged Don't React for Blend In because when everyone else was reacting to jokes all the time, it was best to react along with them. I allowed myself to relax in English like in no other lesson – even though Alan Tydman sat right behind me. I would hear him snorting and whooping and knew that the best way of protecting my back was to do the same. Peter Horn sat next to me and I'm sure in those lessons his stammer improved.

Yes, we were pretty much ready for anything from Mr Smith, but still we were stunned into silence when he announced on Tuesday afternoon, 'Today I'd like to introduce you to an old friend of mine: Icarus!'

We'd all received Icarus feathers. No one had been backward in coming forward second time round. But still we were none the wiser. Who was this Icarus? Why was he playing silly games?

When Mr Smith made his announcement, I think we all went through the same thought process: whoever was planting the Icarus stuff was someone who knew that this lesson was coming. *Coming soon.* Someone who'd read ahead in *Greek Myths for Today.* And which of us would do that? There was only one person who had any reason to. The person who knew that Icarus was coming was the person who'd *planned* for him to come, precisely then. On Tuesday, at five minutes past two.

'Ha ha, Sir. Is he going to fly?' said Alan. '*With feathers?*'

'He is, Mr Tydman!' said Mr Smith, acting shocked and amazed. 'May we deduce from your questions that you have actually read a chapter of *Greek Myths* voluntarily? Voluntarily, by the way, means without being asked. If so, we must celebrate! I shall . . .'

'No, Sir, I haven't read ahead in the book. But I got your note, Sir, thank you, Sir. Nice joke.' All those Sirs were meant to be funny, just like Mr Smith saying 'Mr Tydman'.

'Don't interrupt, Mr Tydman,' he said now, but he seemed momentarily confused. Perhaps he hadn't expected his joke would be exposed so soon.

'We shall celebrate anyway!' he exclaimed suddenly. 'Let's have a round of Just A Minute!'

This was a first. Not that we hadn't played Just A Minute before; we had. We loved it. But before we had always played at the *end* of a lesson. Just A Minute was our reward when Mr Smith was especially pleased with how we'd done. And that was another odd thing: he clearly *wasn't* pleased today. Alan *hadn't* read ahead in the book, there was no cause for celebration.

The puzzle was solved when he went on to say that the subject he'd chosen was the Icarus myth; the first contestant, Alan Tydman.

'Mr Tydman knows Icarus is going to fly: that much he's told us. And to fly, as he put it so eloquently, "with feathers". But what else does he know? Enough to fill a minute? Let's see!'

If you've never played Just A Minute, I'd better break off at this point, to explain the rules. Somebody has to speak on a subject for *just a minute* (which, if it's you, seems more like a year) without hesitation, deviation or repetition. Deviation is changing the subject, or straying away from it by degrees. If you do deviate – or hesitate or repeat a word – you can be challenged. And if the challenge is correct, then the challenger takes the subject from you for what's left of the time. Whoever is speaking when the minute's up is the winner of the round.

Even Peter Horn loved Just A Minute. I mean, a game where you're out if you *hesitate* should have been torture for him, but it wasn't. If he stammered, Mr Smith held up a hand to show it didn't count – and once he *deliberately* stammered near the end, to stretch out his turn and win. We couldn't be sure if it was deliberate, but Mr Smith shouted, 'All's fair in love and war!' which seemed to mean it was. (He apologized later, for using a cliché. He said he'd done it in the heat of the moment. He apologized for that one, too.)

The other surprise, when we played Just A Minute, was Bogsy: he often won. He did it by slowing down his speech, which sounded weird, like a voice recorder gone wrong, but was clever because it gave him more time to think – and fewer words to say. Once he spoke on the subject of 'Peace' for a whole minute without being challenged. Only he didn't: he spoke about *peas*. (Bonus point for inventiveness.) Any of us could have got him for deviation, but no one did, because it was funny. After the lesson, he was got, though: by Alan. Jostled so hard that he nearly fell over. But that was outside, in the corridor. Somehow, in Mr Smith's room, things were different. We all felt safe.

Till the day Mr Smith asked Alan to speak for just a minute about Icarus.

'Beware deviation, Mr Tydman, and good luck!' Glancing up at the classroom clock, Mr Smith rubbed his hands. Then, as the clock's thin red finger swept past twelve, he shouted, 'Go!'

The trouble was, Alan was excited. He thought he had it all sewn up and that Icarus's day was done. He must have felt relieved at the prospect of no more uncertainty – and he over-relaxed. When Mr Smith said 'Go', he jumped up from his chair and stood to attention. Then he laughed and shouted, '*Icarus dickarus!* SIR!'

Mr Smith looked annoyed. Which was pretty restrained, all things considered. 'Alan, you're an idiot,' he said. 'I thought perhaps you weren't, but you are. What a shame. All right, sit down. We'll forget Just A Minute. I thought it might be fun, but I was wrong.' He reached for a whiteboard pen. '*I* don't mind, but the Icarus show must go on, nonetheless.'

Alan was still standing up. He laughed again. 'I'll believe it when I see it, Sir!'

'Sit down, Alan!' No 'Mr Tydman' now. '*I'll* believe in *you* as fit to remain in this class – when you *sit down*.' He was fiddling with the whiteboard pen, as if the lid wouldn't go on. But really he was giving Alan time. It was like when Timmy takes too long in the bathroom, and Mum stands outside and counts to ten . . .

But Alan still didn't sit. He flapped his arms like a baby bird. Mr Smith, intent on his pen lid, didn't see, or at least pretended not to. He was listening for the scrape of Alan's chair.

'Alan, I'm warning you seriously now.' If this were Mum, she'd have reached seven or eight. 'Listen carefully. I'm about to write on the board. While I am writing, you will sit down and tell us – since you clearly know *something* – who you think Icarus is. Then we'll get on.'

He turned to the board and wrote the date.

Underneath it, very slowly, like Mum saying nine and a half, *nine and three quarters*, he wrote:

'Who is Icarus?'

And Alan slipped out of his place and tiptoed towards the front of the class.

We watched.

When he got there, he stopped and yelled, 'YOU ARE, SIR!' Then he pulled his feather out of his pocket and stuck it down the back of Mr Smith's shirt.

When shocking things happen in books and comics, people gasp. It happens quite often. But I'd never heard anyone gasp in real life – till then. When Alan did that, someone actually gasped. I don't know who. Alan waited.

Mr Smith had given a start, but otherwise no reaction.

(Impressive.) In the silence that followed, he spoke very softly, without turning round.

'Beware deviation!' he said. It was scary. 'Do you remember? I warned you, Alan. Deviant behaviour can lose you the game.' He wasn't talking about Just A Minute. I think he was using a metaphor, but I wasn't about to ask. Whether he was or not, it was a threat.

He raised his elbow and reached down his back for Alan's feather, which must have been tickling. He fished about for some time, with no result. Maybe by now it had worked its way into his pants. Somebody sniggered – and that's when he lost it. He whirled round and started shouting. Spit flew right into Alan's face.

'THAT'S IT! I'VE HAD ENOUGH! WHAT'S GOT INTO YOU, ALAN? WHAT'S GOING ON?' He made one last, violent lunge with his arm down his back: the tickle was driving him mad. 'AS FOR YOUR F – . . . AS FOR YOUR *FEATHERS*!'

Alan didn't say a word. The only sound was a small shuffling here and there round the room, as the people who'd thought to take out their own feathers quickly hid them away. Mr Smith heard, and something about the sound seemed to make him give up.

As suddenly as he'd started, he stopped. He gave up trying to fish out the feather. He gave up on it all.

'Triple detention!' he said wearily. 'And if there's any more of this nonsense, there *will* be a note, I assure you – to your parents!' He motioned Alan back to his seat. 'It won't be from me, though, whatever you say. It'll be from the Head!'

So, Icarus wasn't Mr Smith. We learned in the rest of the lesson that he was in fact an ancient Greek boy. Daedalus, his father, was this amazing craftsman. Ever heard of the Labyrinth of the Minotaur? Daedalus built *that*! And when things went wrong for the two of them and they wound up imprisoned together, Daedalus made them each a pair of wings. He used real feathers – and blobs of beeswax for glue – and, Daedalus being Daedalus, they worked! He and Icarus *flew away*. Imagine that. Icarus got so excited about it that he kept on going up, higher and higher. He flew too close to the sun in the end, and the heat of it melted the beeswax. He died because his wings fell apart and he plummeted into the sea.

That was Icarus in the myth. Who it was dishing out notes and feathers, here and now, we still didn't know.

Alan said no more that afternoon. In fact, everyone was silent. Mr Smith had to pick on people when he wanted answers to questions. Peter's stammer, I noticed, was really bad, and I myself felt jumpy. There was danger in the air.

CHAPTER 5

REACTORS AND NON-REACTORS

Alan had got it in the neck from Mr Smith, so someone would get it from Alan. Someone, as he said, was going to get their head screwed off. Because that was the way things worked. Really, it should be the Icarus person, but if Icarus wasn't revealing himself, it would have to be someone else. I knew I must exercise all my skill to make sure it wasn't me.

The way I liked to look at the world was in terms of Reactors and Non-reactors. Non-reactors were the ones who got by; Reactors got hurt. The ultimate example of a Non-reactor was a stone. If you kicked a stone, it ended up just the same, only further down the road. If you kicked, say, Bogsy – well, look what had happened with Alan that first day of term. The stone didn't react to being kicked, and finished up a stone. Bogsy did react, and finished up – Bogsy. Which would *you* model yourself on? See!

Of course, those are two extreme examples. Most things fall somewhere in between. Shadow's not a stone, but she's a definite non-reactor. Timmy isn't Bogsy, but he ought to watch out. I mean, with a name like Timmy Meadows, you're living dangerously, aren't you? Sounds like a character out of *Peter Rabbit*. How much would it take for one of Timmy's friends to call him Squirrel Nutkin? But Timmy doesn't seem to worry about that. He has loads of friends and they're always coming round ours. They make loads of mess – it drives Mum mad – but they've never fallen out. So far. So far, the only variation on Timmy I've heard is Tim.

Thank goodness my name's sensible. Alex Meadows. Alex. It's even a bit like Alan. Nice and safe.

But another of my sayings is Don't Be Complacent. Which means if things are going your way, don't think you can relax, because next minute they may not be. I try never ever to relax, except under special circumstances. One of the special circumstances is when I'm in Don's shed.

I went to Don's shed a lot over the days following Icarus at school. Everyone seemed to be waiting – either for Icarus to make his next move or for Alan to get bored of waiting, and make a move of his own. Nobody wanted to be within range if he did. Nobody wanted to be the one to set him off.

In Don's shed, it was just me – and sometimes Shadow – and a spider or two. Oh, and a brilliant non-reactor that I'd never even seen. The shed was brick, so old that the mortar was crumbling away in places. There were loads of nooks and crannies and even little holes right through the wall. In a gap between two bricks, just under the roof, lived a creature that *nibbled*.

I knew it nibbled because all summer (I mean since we'd moved) I'd heard it. It nibbled something brittle and dry, like burnt toast, only very, very quietly: *much* more quietly than a *person* eating toast could have done. And it went on nibbling no matter what else was going on. If Shadow came in, it went on nibbling, which made me think it couldn't be a mouse because mice are definitely reactors when cats get involved.

Once I climbed on to Don's old chest of drawers to get a closer look. I shone a torch right into the gap where the nibbling was coming from and it didn't even pause. I couldn't *see* anything in there, but the sound was really close. Then one of the chest of drawers legs gave way and the whole thing tilted and I fell off. When the smash-crash was over – and Shadow had bolted – and I'd picked myself up and calmed down – I listened. Yes. You've guessed it! Superb. If Alan himself had come in and gone crazy and thrown things about and twisted my head off, the nibbler would have nibbled on, regardless. It was a reassuring thought.

Don's shed was a reassuring place altogether. I spent my time there relaxing on a pile of old sacks, reading, or sitting on my favourite box, or poking about among Don's stuff. All the serious stuff – his wheelbarrow, his lawnmower, his tools – had been sold. His grown-up son,

Donald, had come back from Australia when he died, and had a big clear out. (That was when Maisie had gone to The Laurels: she'd been cleared out, too.) But Donald had left the things I suppose weren't worth selling: plant pots, tins of rusty old nails, stuff like that. I didn't like the sound of Donald and so made sure I never met him.

There were loads of interesting bits and pieces in the chest of drawers. I was going through them slowly. The day after Icarus Day, I found an old horseshoe and hung it on the door like I know people used to do for good luck. I banged in the nails with a broken brick, which made Shadow run outside. But she came back in and curled up on the sacks when the banging stopped. The nibbler wasn't nibbling that day. In fact, I hadn't heard it for ages. As summer came to an end, it had nibbled less and less and at last – perhaps – gone. But that didn't mean the shed was silent. No such luck. There were plenty of noises from the other side of the wall.

Don's shed stands back to back with our old one – the one that Bogsy's family got when they bought our house. The division between the two gardens runs down between the backs of the sheds. I don't think Bogsy's parents like gardening – they never seem to do any – so the shed, as far as I could tell, became Bogsy's own. I didn't mind him having it. It was only a cheap, flimsy thing that Mum and Dad had bought as a kit. Don's shed is much better, being brick, with a nice brick floor and a proper slate roof.

I hadn't a clue what Bogsy got up to in his shed, any more than he had a clue what I did in mine. I wondered what he thought of my banging. I know what I thought of the noises he made: the scraping and scuffling, the scratching, the bumps. They were irritating. Peculiar. But of course I never react.

The day I found the second blank envelope – slipped inside that pocket in my bag, just like the first – I took it, like the first, to Don's shed. Briefly I imagined Bogsy opening his in *his* shed. I knew he was there because I'd heard him. But then I remembered he was a reactor – he wouldn't care where he opened his, or who saw. He'd probably opened it in the house.

I unsealed mine and took out the slip of white paper. No feather this time. Just the note.

'November 2nd', it said, in computer writing. And underneath, 'Icarus'.

Even though this time I knew I wasn't alone in getting an envelope, I still *felt* alone, sitting there with the note in my hands. I wished the nibbler was around. The spider was, but that was no help. It had spun a new web, I noticed, and was lying in wait, which made everything worse. Again I felt someone was watching me and yet, at the window, there was nobody there.

November 2nd. This was September. In two months, the boy – Icarus – would fly. Now I believed it. The date made it real. But how would he? Why would he? Where? And *who was he*? So much was missing. Icarus held all the cards and he was playing them close to his chest. It struck me that really the thing to do would be try and make a discovery, work something out, instead of waiting for Icarus to throw out crumbs of information. That way, he wouldn't have all the control. But where to start? How to sneak up on him? Those were the questions – the *urgent* questions, because now the clock was ticking.

CHAPTER 6
DO NOTHING

A good place to start would be Maisie, I thought, so on Saturday morning, when I went to The Laurels, I was looking forward to updating her on all that had happened and to asking her opinion. But they told me at the reception desk that she wasn't well enough to see me.

They said that sometimes. They never said what she had or how badly. I was always careful not to react. I always said thank you and left. Today, though, perhaps because I needed her advice, perhaps because I'd decided that I must start doing something myself, I *pretended* to leave, but didn't really. When I was halfway down the drive, I quickly stepped into the bushes (laurels, I suppose) and doubled back towards the building. I felt like a criminal, and hoped they didn't have CCTV.

I crept round the side of the building, where Maisie's room let on to the garden through a pair of French windows, and looked in.

She wasn't in bed, as I'd expected, but sitting in her chair. The back of the chair was towards me, but Maisie's head and shoulders poked up above it. She was dressed, I could see, and not in her nightie, but she was *shaking*. Her shoulders juddered and her head kept tipping forward. It was awful.

For the first time, it occurred to me Maisie might die, like Don. What would I do then?

I came away.

Mum and Dad were talking in the kitchen.

'Don't worry,' said Mum, 'with his *Do Nothing* policy, he won't make a fuss, and anyway you can truthfully say the new one will be an improvement for everyone. Him, too. He'll soon grow to love it. You'll see.'

I opened the door. 'Who're you talking about?' I said.

Mum looked flustered. 'You shouldn't eavesdrop,' she said, 'it's sneaky.'

'Who were you talking about?'

'Alex, you . . . Oh, just – someone,' she said. 'How's Maisie?'

'I wasn't allowed in. She's got the shakes.'

'Is that what they said?'

'No, but I saw. What's wrong with her?'

They looked at each other, puzzled and worried, and Dad said, 'Parkinson's?' Then, to me, 'Parkinson's Disease. Some people get it when they're old. It makes you shake – among other things. Oh dear, poor Maisie.'

'Do you get better?'

'I don't know,' said Dad. 'Probably. But we don't even know if it's definitely that. Maybe it's something else.'

I got myself a pencil and paper and took them down to Don's shed.

The pencil and paper were to make a list. If I couldn't see Maisie – and who knew how long this Parkinson's thing would last – then I'd have to try working things out myself.

I would make a list of everyone I knew, then cross out the names of the people who couldn't possibly be Icarus. Eventually, I'd be left with just one – and the mystery would be solved. It was called a process of elimination. You found reasons to eliminate possibilities and you went on eliminating till you had your answer.

I sat on the old wooden box and got myself a seed tray to press on. At the top of my piece of paper I wrote, 'People Who Could Be Icarus,' and underlined it. Then I wrote, 'Maisie', and immediately crossed her out. Maisie couldn't be Icarus. For a start, I just *knew* she couldn't be Icarus, like I knew that pigs couldn't fly. But the rule was you had to have a reason, not just a feeling. My *reason* for eliminating Maisie was that she didn't have access to a computer (she didn't have access to anything, really) and couldn't possibly have written the notes.

Underneath Maisie, I wrote Donald, and crossed him out, too. My reason for eliminating Donald was that he was in Australia.

This was going well. Underneath Maisie and Donald, I wrote Mum, Dad and Timmy. I crossed out Timmy because of his spelling, but I couldn't think of reasons for Mum and Dad. Of course, I knew neither of them was Icarus but, however strong the feeling, it *was* just a feeling. Then I hit on a fact: Dad was allergic to birds. We couldn't visit Auntie Jen because she had a parrot. (At least, that's why Dad said it was.) That would do for Mum as well, I thought: Mum would never do anything with feathers, in case Dad got a reaction.

After I'd eliminated them, I put down Auntie Jen. Auntie Jen said she wouldn't come to Burstead until we went to Manchester because it was our turn. But we'd never go to Manchester because of Squawky. I could safely cross out Auntie Jen.

Then, encouraged by my success, I wrote down the names of everyone in our form, including Miss McGowan. And that gave me another idea. I added Mr Smith. I was able to cross him off straight away – along with Alan Tydman – because of that clash they'd had in the Icarus lesson. It was like playing Cluedo: Alan had thought Mr Smith was Icarus – so Alan couldn't be Icarus himself – and Mr Smith had thought Alan was barking, so he couldn't be Icarus, either. But after that, I was stuck.

I'd been doing so well. I'd been able to eliminate every single name on my list – till I'd put down the form. Suddenly there were twenty-eight names I hadn't a clue about. And what about the whole year? A hundred and fifty names more! Some not even names, just faces, just row upon row of burgundy sweatshirts displayed in the photos in the Jubilee Hall. What about the *school*? A thousand sweatshirts. Talk about anonymous. This was as good as a dictionary definition.

To cheer myself up, I wrote down my own name and crossed it out. I even wrote down Shadow and crossed out that.

A thump from next door, and a brief clatter. Bogsy. Up to his tricks, whatever they were. I went to his name and put a hard, sharp line through it. He'd had a feather that first time, same as me.

I tried to remember who else had been able to produce one when Alan had gone round questioning people. One or two I could picture, holding them up – Andy P, holding his, had been really excited – but mostly my memory was hazy. Had Peter Horn got one? I couldn't be sure. He didn't *seem* like an Icarus type, but really I knew very little about him.

I realized I didn't know anyone, not really. How could you tell what a person was like, inside? By being their friend, I supposed, but my Trust No One policy meant I was friends with no one. For the first time, I felt that there could be drawbacks to that.

CHAPTER 7

NOVEMBER 2ND

I'd begun the process of elimination enthusiastically – but then I'd got discouraged. The process had shown that I couldn't assume Icarus was even someone whose real name I knew. Even if I put down the names of everyone in the whole world I'd ever *heard* of, he (or she) might not be among them. Maisie had pointed out this wasn't personal. Icarus might be a stranger who'd decided to distribute a load of messages like junk mail.

The only thing the list had achieved was to make me different from the Do Nothing person Mum and Dad had talked about in the kitchen. No one could accuse *me* of doing nothing to try to solve the problem.

I went back to Maisie, and this time they let me in.

There was no sign of any more shaking. When I made an ever so casual reference to Parkinson's Disease, she said crossly, 'So you think I've got Parkinson's, do you? Well, you're wrong. Now.'

I didn't argue. I was just pleased to hear her sounding so sure.

I told her about November 2nd, but the date didn't mean anything to her. It got her quite excited, though.

'I'd like to be there!' she said. 'To see the show!'

'So would I,' I said. 'But *where*? Where is "there"?'

'Yes, I see. That's a point. But he's bound to say soon, this Icarus fellow. I must say, I like his style. Wonder who he is?'

Before I left, I promised to tell Don to check if the apples (she called them the Bramleys) were ripe. If they were, he should pick them. 'But tell him to mind how he goes up that ladder. If he falls and breaks his neck, it won't matter how many apples he's picked and it won't matter how many pies I bake . . .' She paused and seemed suddenly uncertain. '. . . there'll be – no one – to eat them.'

The next thing that happened was like in that fairy story called *Rumpelstiltskin*. You know, where the girl has to guess the little man's name or he'll get her baby? She has three days to think of the name, and for the first two, she goes round asking people for ideas and gets loads, but none of them right. Then, on the third day, she kind of gives up. She goes for a walk in the woods, and comes to a clearing and hears someone singing. It's the little man, singing a song *about his name*! (Would you sing that song, in his position? You would not. But there, everyone's different.) Of course, it's Rumpelstiltskin. So the girl gets to keep her baby and Rumpelstiltskin gets into a rage and stamps his foot so hard that a hole opens up underneath him and he falls through it, right down to Hell. Which, it turns out, is where he came from.

The point is, the thing that the girl had been trying and trying to work out just sort of plopped into her lap when she'd *stopped* trying because she thought it was hopeless.

The thing *I'd* been trying to work out plopped into *my* lap in a similar way. It happened like this.

Morning registration was running late because Lydia

and Candy had fallen out, and we all had to know about it. Candy asked Miss McGowan if she could be moved because Lydia smelled. Lydia asked if *she* could be moved because Candy's smell was so bad it had spread out from Candy to fill that whole bit of the room. Miss McGowan knew better than to try to get to the bottom of things: it wouldn't have been worth it. She'd learned from experience to take the short cut.

'Right,' she said now. 'Candy, you will move.' She scanned the room for empty places. There was only one. 'Quick! Go and sit next to David, if you can't behave where you are.'

Candy screeched, 'Eurgh! Miss, he smells worse than her! I'm not moving next to *him*!'

'Oh, don't be ridiculous, Candy! Stay where you are, then, and grow up.' She was anxious to get the register done: it was nearly quarter to nine. And just then, there was a knock on the door. A loud, jaunty knock, which beat out the good old rhythm of 'Shave and a hair cut'.

Bom b-b-bom bom!

Miss McGowan's face flushed, maybe from irritation,

maybe something else. Her response was drowned out by ours – the traditional one. We all stamped or banged out the rhythm of 'Two bits!'

BOM BOM!

The door opened. Only one person could make such an entrance.

'Was that "Come in"?' said Mr Smith.

People said Mr Smith and Miss McGowan fancied each other.

'Hello, you horrible lot!' he said to us, and to her, 'Can I have a quick word, please, outside?' He backed out into the corridor, without giving her time to reply.

Everyone went, 'WOOOO!'

Miss McGowan looked flustered. 'We *must* get the register finished,' she said desperately. 'Someone must come up and finish it while I'm gone.' She looked at her laptop. It just so happened that mine was the last name she'd called – and I was sensible enough.

'Alex!' she said. 'Come and sit at my desk. You can do it. Hurry up, though – I won't be long.'

'That's right, miss,' shouted Alan. 'Just a quickie!'

She fled. And I, all unknowing, was set on a course for the hidden clearing where Rumpelstiltskin would sing his song.

Whether or not Alan was right, I had plenty of time. The job was easy. Miss McGowan had already got halfway through. Before I'd even sat down in her chair and pulled her laptop towards me, I knew there was only one absentee. I knew this without even checking, because of the one vacant seat we'd all seen when Candy was going to have to move. I put another 'A' at the end of the line of 'A's after Chloë Prelutsky's name. Some people said she'd got cancer, but some said her parents had taken her to Florida because it was cheaper to go in term time (though you did get a letter from the Head).

I put slashes for everyone else, and then I was done.

I wondered if I should go back to my place, but decided not. It's not every day you get to sit in a teacher's chair, and I liked it. No one was taking any notice of me. Candy and Lydia were so excited at the thought of Miss McGowan and Mr Smith that they'd made up.

I looked at the laptop again. Chloë Prelutsky had been

absent since September 21st. You could tell straight away, just by reading up to the line of dates at the top of the screen.

There were dates running down the side, too, beside all our names. Random dates that dotted about through the year, not the neat progression – September 21st, 22nd and so on – across the top. One of these random ones caught my eye. March 30th. My birthday. And sure enough, when I read across: Alex Meadows, followed by a row of slashes.

So they were birthdays. That was more fun. I ran my eye down the list, from the top, to see if anyone had theirs coming up soon. November 21st, July 8th, December 25th (wow, imagine having a birthday on Christmas Day – that was Peter Horn – I never knew *that*), November 2nd . . .

November 2nd.

The door of the classroom opened and Miss McGowan came back in. Everyone whistled and wooo-ed again, except me. Everyone would be looking to see if her lipstick was smudged or her hair messed up. But not me.

She clapped her hands for quiet and said, 'Thank you, Alex. You've done well. Now go back to your place . . . Come on, Alex, wake up!'

I pushed myself out of her chair and caught my leg on the corner of her desk. I was dimly aware of her saying, 'Careful, Alex. Are you all right?' but I couldn't have replied. I blundered away and sat down.

I'd read across to the name for that date.

I didn't dare raise my eyes, in case they met *his* and he guessed that I knew.

The name for November 2nd was David Marsh.

Bogsy.

CHAPTER 8

CAN YOU BELIEVE IT?

So Bogsy was Icarus. Icarus was Bogsy. I couldn't believe it. *Bogsy* was Bogsy. Useless. A loser. An outcast. Everything I myself would never be. Maybe the birthday was just a coincidence. But no, I knew it wasn't that. *Somebody* had to be Icarus and maybe an outsider wasn't so surprising. Bogsy was an oddball, and sending those notes and feathers was – well, you couldn't get much odder than that.

After I'd calmed down, I studied Bogsy when he wasn't looking. Everything about his *appearance* was normal. He was medium-sized – not fat, not thin – lank hair, a serious mouth. I couldn't remember him smiling ever, but then I couldn't remember him ever having much to smile about.

Why should I find it hard to believe that a useless person like him should be doing something useless? That's what useless people did.

But the truth was, the Icarus stuff *wasn't* useless, not really.

Not at all. There was something – bold – about it. The idea of somebody flying was great. What had been far and away the best story in *Greek Myths for Today*? OK, it all ended badly, but up until then, till the beeswax melted, who wouldn't have swapped places with Icarus and gone soaring into the sky?

Maisie had said she liked his style. And she hadn't been talking about the flying. She'd been talking about the feathers, the anonymous notes, the teaser campaign. There *was* something stylish about it, agreed. Imagine daring to do all that on your own, without telling Alan. Imagine doing it *to* Alan – knowing that your life wouldn't be worth living if you got found out.

But doing it anyway.

What would that feel like? What must Bogsy be feeling now?

Then you *are* found out. Just a few chapters in, along comes – not Sherlock Holmes, but little old me! Just some random person. Bumbling about in the woods (metaphorically speaking) I strike gold. I discover Bogsy's secret. Everyone knows he's not normal, but only I know *how* not normal he is. So now I know more than the others – more, even, than Bogsy, who doesn't know I know. I have power. And the question is what am I going to do with it?

Don't React. I tried out my favourite motto. What did it mean in this situation? Don't let anything show, that was obvious, but what then? Act Normal.

Once before, I'd had power – or thought I had. That time I'd seen Bogsy go after the feather at the bus stop and assumed he'd received it the same way as me. (Joke! His whole bag had most likely been stuffed full of feathers! The only surprise was that none had ever escaped before.)

What did I do then? I acted normal. I told Alan.

Act Normal now. Tell Alan again. He might be impressed – he might even be grateful. His gang would respect me and welcome me in. I'd never need worry again.

And Alan would get Bogsy. Do for him properly. Was I worried about that? Icarus would be stuffed. Well, it couldn't be helped. That's what I told myself, anyway. What did I care if he never got off the ground?

Looking back now, it's painfully clear: I was lying.

At break, I followed Alan and the others to the science wall. That was where Alan operated from. When we got there, I dared to stand closer to him than usual. It was exciting. But I wouldn't tell him now. I'd await my moment.

The first thing that happened was Andy P came round the corner.

Why did he do it, I wondered – keep trying? Why not accept things the way they were? He was one up from Bogsy.

He held out his money. 'One, please, Al.'

'For you?' said Alan.

Andy seemed to hesitate slightly. He'd had an idea. Then he said, 'No, for Tom.'

Alan noticed the hesitation but couldn't work out what it meant. He nodded to Rob. Rob fished about in their special backpack and brought out a little white bag, which he handed to Alan, and which Alan tossed to Andy. You could tell from the way it arced through the air and the way that Andy caught it, it was full. He looked really pleased.

'Thanks, Al.' He thought he was making progress.

When he'd gone, 'What's the date?' said Alan, all casual, to no one in particular.

'October 5th,' said Rob, and then added, 'Four weeks to go.'

'Why d'you say that?' snapped Alan. 'Four weeks till what?' He knew, but he wanted someone to say.

'Funday!' said someone else – it was Jack Tweedy – and somebody sniggered.

'What d'you mean, Funday?' said Alan. Of course, he knew.

'You know, *Fun*day,' said Jack. 'November 2nd. When we all look up into the sky and get to see who's been laughing at us.'

'*FUNDAY?*' Alan shouted suddenly. Then he got sweary and shouted other things as well. He stepped close to Jack and shouted them all, right in his face. It was like when Mr Smith had shouted at *him*. You could see the spit. But Jack didn't dare wipe it off, any more than Alan had that day in English. '*November 2nd?*' he went on. More swearing. 'It makes me *sick*! And if anyone mentions *Bird Boy* again, I'm gonna screw their head off!'

There was silence.

And that's when Tom Flynn and Damien came round the wall.

'Anything left, Al?' said Tom. He held out a coin.

'*Anything left?*' said Alan, finding it hard to stop shouting (and not really trying). 'Anything left, after what you've just had?'

Tom looked confused.

'You want to watch out, you do, Tom,' said Alan. 'You've got a problem. An – *eating disorder*.'

He took another white bag from Rob, but this time tipped it straight out on the ground. Shiny, foil-wrapped

70

toffees fell round his feet. When he handed the bag to Tom, there can only have been one or two left inside.

Tom seemed about to protest, but Alan said loudly, 'We don't want you getting *fat*, do we?' and Tom and Damien left, without a word. Tom was middle ranking – well above Bogsy and Andy P – but he wasn't that bothered about the Battalion, not really. He and Damien had each other and could take it or leave it. He cut his losses, on this occasion, with barely a shrug.

No one came forward to pick up the sweets, although they were good ones and would have been fine, being wrapped. Nobody moved. This was my moment. This was when *I* stepped forward and said, *I know who he is, Alan – Bird Boy.*

It would have been perfect. *I know who Icarus is.*

Electrifying.

All I had to do was speak up and make my short announcement.

There was only one problem.

I didn't want my head screwed off.

My discovery seemed to change everything. For a start, it washed all my mottos away. By not telling Alan at break that day, I wasn't Acting Normal. All right, no one fancies their head being screwed off – but I hadn't told him at lunchtime, either, when he'd calmed down, nor on the bus home. I could even have sent him an Icarus style note: *Icarus is Bogsy.* Signed: *A Friend.* Then, when he wanted to know who to thank, I could have come forward. But I didn't.

You could say I Wasn't Reacting. That's what I said to myself, at first. It made me feel safer, to think I was just going on as I always had. But I knew that the old me would have told Alan by now. This wasn't Not Reacting. It wasn't doing nothing. Keeping quiet about Bogsy was something else.

Even Trust No One didn't work any more. Like with Don't React, I could kid myself that that was what I was doing. But if I was honest, I had to admit that by keeping quiet I was trusting *someone*. I was giving him what I think Mum would have called 'the benefit of the doubt'. That meant you let a person go ahead with whatever it was, in the belief that it might – just *might* – turn out worthwhile.

I didn't know what Icarus was up to, but if I stopped him, I never would.

CHAPTER 9
MARBLES

'I've come to see Maisie,' I said to the woman behind the reception desk of The Laurels. 'Shall I just go straight through?' I was being firm, starting forward as I spoke, because I could see she was hesitating and I really didn't want to be turned away.

But before she could open her mouth to say anything, a loud, wailing sob burst out somewhere behind her.

'No,' she said hurriedly. 'Maisie's not well again. Sorry. Come back next week.'

She didn't say anything about the sob, which had given way to a series of choking moans, not as loud as the first one, but continuous and terrible. Someone was really upset in there. The sound made me think of the sound

Timmy made when Shadow had got his hamster and he found it chewed up on the lawn.

'Goodbye,' said the woman, and then again, 'Sorry.' She was nervous.

I didn't believe Maisie was ill this time. They just wanted to get rid of me, in case I decided to tell someone that the old people in The Laurels were badly treated. I could tell the papers.

'Bye,' I said meaningfully, swivelled round slowly and walked out. As soon as I felt she couldn't see me any longer, I dived into the bushes and came back under cover, as I'd done before.

Maisie's French windows were double-glazed. I couldn't hear anything from inside. But I could see Maisie, in her chair as before and – yes – she was shaking. This time, though, I wasn't going away. Even if Maisie was ill, she wasn't that ill: she wasn't in bed. And anyway, ill people *especially* need visitors. Maisie especially needed me right now because I could talk to her, tell her something interesting, at least take her mind off that horrible crying she'd have to sit listening to otherwise.

I tapped on the glass. Nothing happened. Maisie's head and shoulders, above the back of her chair, went on shaking. I hoped her illness wasn't catching, and tried the handle of the window. It was locked.

I banged on the glass, quite loud. This time, she suddenly stopped shaking. I watched her push herself out of her chair and turn round.

She hadn't got spots or a rash. Nothing like that. But all round her eyes was swollen, so the eyes themselves looked unusually small, and her whole face was glistening, as if the skin was oozing moisture. I almost wished I hadn't come, but it was too late for that now.

She came across to the French windows and tried the fastening from the inside, but couldn't make it open. She jabbed a finger towards the room next to hers and turned and went out through the door.

I went where she'd pointed. I could see through the glass of the door that I came to, it wasn't exactly a room, more of a cupboard, with shelves on either side and this narrow glass door at the end, where I waited. The door said, EMERGENCY ONLY, in big red letters.

Maisie arrived on the inside and pushed down a horizontal bar, which opened the door. 'Come on,' she said and I followed her back to her room.

The sobbing had stopped. All I could hear was the sound of a TV in a room down the corridor – Maisie's own was switched off – and a sudden, loud, bubbling parp, which was Maisie blowing her nose.

'Someone was crying,' I said.

She blew again. 'Yes.' She mopped her face with her hankie. 'It was me.'

'*You?*'

It's always embarrassing when adults cry, and especially when you know them. I wanted to change the subject at once, *deviate* from it as soon as I could, but also I was curious.

'Is it your illness?' I said.

It wasn't.

'How many times do I have to tell you?' she burst out. 'I – am – not – ill!'

'What, then?' I said. 'Why *were* you – crying?'

'Well, why do people usually cry?'

I shrugged. 'Because they're sad?'

She gave me a look with eyebrows raised, her nearest thing to a nod.

'But why?' I said. 'Why are you sad?'

'Because –'

I could see she was really unsure of herself. Then she got it together.

'Because Don – died.'

Suddenly I felt sad, too. Terribly sad. Of course, for months I'd known Don was dead, but when she said that, in that room, where we'd talked just last week about how he must gather the apples, it was like he'd died again. I wondered if Maisie thought he'd only *just* died, or if she knew the whole truth – and which would be worse.

'Who told you?' I said. Whoever it was, they shouldn't have done. She'd been happy, believing in Don.

'Oh, nobody *told* me,' she said. 'It's been coming upon me for a while.' I remembered how she had faltered at the thought of Don up the tree and falling and not being there any more to eat her homemade apple pies. 'Now I know for sure, like – you know – like night follows day and eggs are eggs. He died this summer. But –' she dropped her voice confidentially – 'it's a funny thing: sometimes I think he's still here.'

'Yes, I know.'

'Just shows the tricks a lonely old woman can play on herself.'

I wondered if that meant I'd helped to trick her, by going along with the stuff about Don, by saying I'd take messages to him. When she told me to tell him to leave the tomatoes, should I have said, Maisie, there are no tomatoes? When she told me to tell him to take care on the ladder, should I have said, Look, don't worry, he's already dead?

And then: if I'd tricked her over Don, would she think I'd made Icarus up, as well? I was not to be trusted! Why should one be real, but not both? (And how strange that the one that *was* real – the flying boy – was so much less believable than the other – the old man picking tomatoes.)

'Maisie,' I said cautiously, 'do you remember that boy

I told you about, who reckons he's going to fly?'

'Rubbish!' she said, and my heart sank. But then, 'No boy is going to fly. I told you before.'

'You do remember, though? About the feathers? The notes? The date?'

'Of course I remember! What d'you take me for? I haven't lost all my marbles, you know!'

When she looked at me then, I saw with relief that her eyes were pretty much back to normal. The skin at the corners went into all its old creases when she added, 'But I may have lost one or two: I can't remember what date you said.'

'November 2nd. And guess what? I found out what's important about it! I came to tell you. I know who Icarus is!'

She listened while I said about the register and the list of birthdays. When I'd finished, her hand went up to her necklace. She held it for most of the rest of the conversation.

'Well, well. Fancy it being your friend next door all along!'

'He's not my friend, I keep telling you,' I said.

'Well, who is, then?'

The question didn't seem relevant. Must be those missing marbles, I thought, and I twisted it round in my head, to one I preferred.

'He hasn't got any friends,' I said.

'Ah. A loner, is he? That fits. Loneliness can make crazies of us all.'

Speak for yourself, I wanted to say, but it wouldn't have been kind, so I didn't. Nonetheless, suddenly feeling uncomfortable, I started to leave. She pushed me back into my chair so hard that my feet came right up off the floor, like in a cartoon.

She was frowning with concentration. 'Alex,' she said, and that was unusual, she rarely began a sentence with that. 'Alex, I'm worried.'

'So am I. I might miss lunch!'

She ignored me. 'If, as you say, it's *him*, then you ought to tell someone.' She seemed to be squeezing her necklace now. Her knuckles were white.

'I have. You!'

'Someone else, I mean. Someone at school. A teacher. When people are larking about, that's one thing, but when they're not, that's another. You have to consider their motivation.'

This was getting silly.

'He's just putting on a show! You said so yourself! You wanted to go! It'll be like a circus act or something . . .'

She shook her head. 'This boy's no clown.'

He certainly wasn't. Anyone less like a clown than Bogsy was hard to imagine. I smiled. But I couldn't see what she was getting at and felt disappointed in her. Before, it had been as if she and I had been doing a jigsaw together. I'd brought her the pieces, one by one, and she'd fitted them in and got excited. Now, for no good reason, she wanted to throw it all away. Perhaps there were more marbles missing than I'd thought.

'I'm off now,' I said, and slipped out of my chair and past her, to the door. This time she didn't try to stop me, but repeated her thing about how I must go to a teacher.

'D'you want me to take any messages home, for Mum or Dad? *Or anyone else?*'

I needed to distract her, and that line popped into my head. Leading her on like that was a trick, no question: I shouldn't have done it. Especially as she'd just told me she'd finally realized the truth about Don. I half hoped she wasn't going to fall for it – but she did. She let go of her necklace.

'Yes! Tell Don, when he picks the apples, to line the shelves with paper. Tell him to make sure the apples don't touch when he puts them out, because if they touch –' she stuffed her limp, wet hankie up her sleeve – 'and one of them goes, they all will. Now.'

I said OK, though I didn't understand. It was only pretend, after all.

'Better go out the same way you came in,' said Maisie, checking to see that the corridor was clear, 'or we might be in trouble!'

'Maisie's not ill,' I told Mum and Dad. 'They were lying, down at The Laurels.'

'I'm sure they weren't,' said Mum. 'They're responsible adults. She must have been ill and now she's better. Well, I'm glad.'

'No, she wasn't ill in the first place. Just sad. About Don.' I lowered my voice. 'She was *crying*.'

'Oh dear,' said Mum. 'Poor Maisie.'

'But she's fine again now. Now she's gone back to thinking he's still alive, and she's OK.' I was telling myself that my trick had made her better, I know I was. Anyway, it was supposed to be the end of the conversation. I didn't want to mention the marbles, how Maisie had inexplicably changed her mind. (They might have asked what she'd changed her mind *about*.) But Dad got there anyway, though he put it in different words. He was tapping his head.

'No one's really OK – up here – if they can believe something like that. That's what they must have meant, at The Laurels: she isn't well in her mind.'

'You don't understand. It's not right,' I said, 'to talk about well and ill: they don't matter. Happy and sad are what matter, and if Maisie's happy, she's OK.'

Mum looked at me then. 'Yes,' she said, 'perhaps. But whatever is going on in her head, it might be better if it weren't. When someone's got something *physically* wrong, then there's more of a chance you can help.'

CHAPTER 10

ALEX IN WONDERLAND

In amongst all the things that had changed when I found out Icarus was Bogsy was this: the way I felt about what I heard through the wall, as I sat in Don's shed. Before, the noises from Bogsy's side had annoyed me. Now, when I heard them, I tried to imagine *what he was doing*. I began to be eaten up by the need to know.

So, on Monday morning, I missed the school bus. I ran up just as the door was closing behind Bogsy. I'd timed it well. I shouted and waved at the driver to stop, but he pretended not to see – as I'd known he would. He was mean, that driver, and hated us all. As the bus pulled away, several faces looked out through the windows – one was Alan Tydman's – and laughed, but I couldn't be bothered to put on my Stupid Me act. I'd get the B17 to school and it came in twenty minutes. I didn't have long.

I made myself wait at the stop till the school bus was finally out of sight, then I nipped back home. Dad's car had gone – which was good – and a big banana-coloured one was parked in its place. Good again. Mum's a physiotherapist and sees patients at home, in her and Dad's bedroom: she must have had an early appointment this morning, which meant she'd be occupied upstairs, at the front of the house. I could safely slip round the side and down the garden without being seen.

The fence between our garden and Bogsy's comes to an end before it gets to the sheds. Way back, it was put up by Don, and I think he must have run out of wood. When we lived in our old house and Don and Maisie were next door, we never minded the gap. If Don was digging in their garden and he saw me in ours, he'd sometimes come through – to give me a stripy snail shell or an interesting bit of old china.

'Alex,' he'd say, 'here's a thing. You don't see a thing

like this every day.' Actually, thinking about it and knowing how much digging he did, *he* probably did – but I was always grateful to have whatever it was, for my collection.

Nowadays, the gap in the fence is filled by our wheelie bins, ours and the Marshes', all in a line, green, blue and black, and there's only a way through once a week, when some are taken out front for the wheelie bin people to come and empty.

I hadn't planned it, but I was lucky: today was wheelie-bin day. The black and the blue had gone, and the green ones stood alone and gappy, like witches' teeth. I crept between them and poked my head out on Bogsy's side. I didn't know what *his* parents did in the morning; I'd have to be careful not to be seen. But there wasn't anyone in the garden or at any of the windows of the house overlooking it. I ran out, trying to keep low to the ground, and let myself into their shed. I pulled the door shut behind me and took in the scene.

And the scene was this: lit by the shed's one window, set high up in the end wall opposite me – a huge, an astonishing, a *magnificent*, mess. The floor was littered with chewing gum wrappers, the ceiling was stuck with drawing pins and nails, from which odd bits of string dangled down. Bogsy had brought in a table and chair and they – and every other raised surface (some shelves, a toolbox, the top of a big white chest freezer) – were covered with paint pots, balls of string, jam jars, paint-brushes, orange peel, apple cores, packets of gum. In amongst all the stuff on the table, I noticed last week's maths homework. He hadn't handed it in, but he'd done it – all the way down to the bottom of the sheet. I'd got stuck (it was really hard) and handed mine in with the second half blank. I hadn't known Bogsy was so good at maths.

There was junk everywhere and yet there was nothing, so far as I could see, to do with flying. Unless you counted a tattered old kite propped up against the wall behind Bogsy's bike. That wall was remarkable for something else.

That wall, despite the gloom of the shed, was a shimmering mass of suns!

Bogsy had painted it all kinds of brilliant reds and yellows, in a pattern of circles. No, not circles: each one was a *spiral* – and a spiral not painted, as you'd expect, from the centre outwards, but from the outside in. I could tell because the paint was always thickest round the edge. Bogsy must have loaded his brush, then gone round and round, getting smaller and smaller, tighter and tighter, paler and paler, till the paint ran out and the circle was too small to see. It was clever, that, the way he'd got the two things to happen simultaneously every time, no matter what size the spiral was – big or small – to begin with. At the centre of each there was nothing. Pop! All gone! (As Mum used to say when Timmy was little and had finished his food.) Empty air – or you could think of it as the light at the end of a tunnel.

One odd one out, though, I noticed. One of the spirals, bizarrely, had fixed at its centre a cardboard tube – from a roll of kitchen foil or something. The tube stuck straight out from the wall and, perhaps because it was just at eye level, I stepped forward, parting a way through the litter with my toe, to look through.

I'm not sure what I expected to see. If I'd been thinking straight: darkness, nothing, the blackness of inside the tube. But if I'd been thinking straight, I wouldn't have put my eye to it at all. What I actually saw was: light! This was a cardboard tunnel with light at the end. A slot of light, like a miniature letterbox. There must be a hole in the wall of the shed. I took my eye away briefly, to see. The wood of the wall had quite a few holes in it, knot holes – and, yes, here was one of them, slightly enlarged to fit the tube. It held the tube snugly. The tube, I now saw, poked right through.

But if the tube and the hole were round (as they were), how could I have seen a *rectangle* of light? I looked again. There it was: horizontal, rather rough at the edges but a definite slot. There must be two holes, one round, one straight-edged; the tube went through the first and butted up to the second. I already knew what the second hole went through, and why it was shaped like that. Bogsy's shed stood back to back with – Don's.

The two stood so close that they touched. Bogsy's shed was wood and had knot holes; Don's shed was brick, getting old and crumbly, and had holes where chunks of mortar were missing. Whoever looked through this tube, looked through one of those holes. Right into Don's shed. Which meant only one thing.

Bogsy was a spy.

Oh, and one other: he spied on me.

I *so* nearly pulled out the tube! I managed to stop myself just in time. I remembered I mustn't do anything that could let him know I'd been here.

Bogsy was a spy. No wonder I'd always had that feeling. It wasn't someone at the window, it wasn't the spider, nor even the nibbler. All the time it was him.

Bogsy was a spy, but that wasn't all. There was something else. What? Why didn't I despise him for doing what he'd done? He'd spotted that two holes – one through wood, one through bricks – were exactly aligned, and he'd set this up. I *couldn't* despise him because it was brilliant! I looked through again.

I wanted to see what Bogsy could see, beyond the end of the tube. I guessed I'd be able to look right across to the cobwebby window, which faced the back wall – maybe spy on the spider. But it turned out I couldn't. There was something in the way.

The thing in the way was the back of someone's head.

For a moment, in my confusion, I felt I *was* Bogsy – I'd wanted to see what he saw, after all – looking in on myself. But Alex Meadows didn't have cropped grey hair and a freckly bald patch. Dad was balding a bit on top, but this wasn't Dad. The head turned slightly, and I saw the shape of the nose (rather hooked) and cheekbones (pointy). I recognized those. But this didn't make sense.

It was Don.

Don, who had died that summer, whose funeral I'd been to, was back in his shed. Dead people are beyond reach, gone forever, yet one had made it back and here he was, not much further away from me than the length of a kitchen foil tube. He didn't look dead, only still. Although I couldn't see his eyes, I knew they'd be open and alive.

And I wasn't frightened, not one little bit. I'd never seen a ghost before, but obviously ghosts are supposed to be scary. Don in Don's shed amongst all Don's things just seemed comfortable and right. Seeing him there made me realize how much I'd missed him.

And then he yawned and rubbed his forehead. The sound and the gesture were both so real, so *un*ghostly, they gave me another idea. What if he wasn't a visiting ghost? What if *I* was? What if Bogsy's tube was a wormhole going through to a parallel world? Alice fell down a rabbit hole into Wonderland, after all. What if Maisie lived here, in this Wonderland world, without anyone knowing? That would explain a lot. She was right to believe Don was still alive because, here, *he was*! Believing in ghosts was more Timmy's style, but Don in a parallel universe was cool.

Did that mean I'd lost my marbles? Dad would say so. He'd say anyone who could believe such stuff wasn't right in the head. But you have to believe your own eyes – and here was Don, in front of mine.

I suddenly feared I'd spent much more time in Bogsy's shed than I'd meant to. So, carefully rearranging the chewing gum wrappers as I went, I backed to the door. I let myself out and slipped back between the bins.

No time to go and peep in at the door of Don's shed, even if I had wanted to. Which I didn't. Without looking over my shoulder, I ran up our garden and round the side of the house. All was well: the big yellow car was still there.

I caught the B17 to school by the skin of my teeth.

CHAPTER 11
STAY-IN-BED-OWS

'Wakey wakey!' sneered Alan Tydman when I opened the classroom door. Miss McGowan shushed him.

Everyone was in their place. Everyone was looking at me.

'You're late, Alex Meadows,' said Miss McGowan.

'Alex Stay-in-Bed-ows,' called Jack Tweedy, and everyone laughed.

'Be quiet!' Miss McGowan snapped. 'Alex, you're late, but you're lucky. I haven't yet got to your name in the register, so you won't be marked absent. I gather you missed the bus: don't do it again. Right. Quickly. Sit down.'

I wondered who had told her. I glanced at Bogsy, but it

wasn't his style. As I passed Alan Tydman, he whispered, 'Alex Bed-ows!' and I knew.

But I didn't care. I'd discovered a parallel universe in a little old garden shed! Who could care about Alan Tydman – or Jack Tweedy and his stupid names – after that? Even Icarus could wait. (Maybe Icarus *came* from the parallel universe! Bogsy's tube was the link, after all. Maybe Bogsy knew all about it and that's how he dared to behave as he did!)

Miss McGowan could get cross and tell me *Don't miss the bus again or else* – but it made no difference. Nothing and no one was going to stop me missing it tomorrow. I couldn't wait to see Maisie's face when I told her I'd seen Wonderland!

Alan Tydman's face was a picture. He couldn't believe Alex Stay-in-Bed-ows had overslept *again*. As the bus pulled away from the stop and poor old Bed-ows came running up, he made Special Needs gestures out of the window.

I didn't go back home this time. When the school bus had disappeared from sight, I crossed the road to the opposite stop, and waited for the B17 in the other direction. My plan would make me *seriously* late for school, but that didn't matter. When the B17 arrived, I got on and was carried into town.

The first thing I saw in The Laurels car park was the big banana car that had been parked outside ours yesterday. It seemed a good sign. See, it seemed to be saying, you're right! The world is full of surprises. You're right to believe in incredible things.

I didn't waste time calling in at reception. That would be stupid. I went straight round to Maisie's French windows. She could let me in through EMERGENCY ONLY just as before.

But when I peered into her room, I saw she had a visitor already. The two of them sat talking, with their chairs pulled together and their heads bent close.

And I saw who the visitor was. All the way from Wonderland, he'd come. He'd come to her and saved her the trouble of having to go to him.

It was Don.

I was starting to tiptoe away, when he looked up. I'd not meant to disturb them. But now he was moving towards the window, beckoning me in. I wondered if the difficult fastening would magically yield to his touch, but it didn't. He had to thump it – hard – with his fist, to make it budge. And then, when it did, and the window opened, he called, 'Don't go! You're Alex, aren't you?' and it wasn't Don's voice, but the voice of a much younger man. His face was very like Don's but, again – yes – younger, and so was his body: younger than Don's, I saw that now, not bent and stiff.

'Donald!' called Maisie from inside the room. 'Will he come? Tell him not to be silly!'

'Ma says don't be silly,' he said, and gave me a smile. I didn't smile back but I followed him back in.

He'd just arrived from Australia, he said, once he'd found me a chair and Maisie had given me a biscuit. His body clock was all over the place: he kept waking up in the middle of the night.

'Yesterday I was coming to see Ma – I was really

excited –' Maisie tutted, but I saw she was pleased – 'when I suddenly realized it was eight in the morning. So I stopped off –'

'At our house,' I filled in.

'Yes. The lights were on and the curtains were open. I thought it would be OK. You'd just left for school, your mum said, and your dad had already gone to work.'

'I think I saw your car,' I said, 'as the school bus went past.'

He laughed. 'I bet you did. Great big monstrosity of a thing: no one could miss it! All they had left in the hire place when I went.'

'Your mum made my boy a nice cup of tea –'

It was funny, Maisie calling him a boy.

'– and you'll never guess where he drank it!'

I will, I thought.

'In Don's shed!'

Donald smiled. 'Not that your mum didn't ask me to sit in the kitchen – I like the new colour, by the way – I just had a sudden real urge to see the old shed. When I was your age, I used to spend more time in there than I did in the house! Used to smoke down there, where Dad and Ma wouldn't see.'

'Oh, hush!' said Maisie. 'Don't go giving Alex ideas. You've more sense than to smoke, haven't you, Alex? A deal more sense that this great booby! And if you think –' she turned to the booby – 'if you think we didn't see . . . Well! The smoke used to pour out through all the gaps in the brickwork. You couldn't have signalled more clearly if you'd tried! Don and I used to stand at the kitchen window, laughing!'

Donald must have heard the story before, because he didn't seem surprised. He just said, 'Anyway, I enjoyed sitting down in the old place again.'

'It's very untidy, he says,' said Maisie severely, frowning at me.

'Ma! I said it's very like Dad had it!'

'Same difference,' said Maisie.

'Well, anyway,' said Donald. 'It is. *Very* like. A bit more mortar gone, that's all. I suppose the mason bees have been at it again – one or two always used to move in in the summer. Sometimes you could actually hear them, chomping away, when the weather was warm. If Dad were alive . . . but there, everyone has their own ideas and your mum's might seem drastic but I have to admit . . .'

At this point, Maisie had a sudden coughing fit. I fetched her a glass of water while Donald thumped her back. He was really quite rough. But then, *she* was quite rough with *him* – in what she said – like calling him a booby. It's funny, how roughness and rudeness can mean you don't care for someone, but also the opposite. I suddenly realized that Donald was talking about Don being dead and it was OK, Maisie wasn't crying. Perhaps it was better that Donald was Donald, after all, not Don-in-a-parallel-world. Perhaps if Maisie had Donald, she could let Don go.

'Um, Donald, how long are you staying?' I asked. 'How long till you have to go back to Australia?'

'Don't know,' said Donald, and Maisie looked away.

CHAPTER 12
INVISIBLE

There'd been something wrong with the conversation I'd had with Maisie and Donald – not the whole of it, just the bit towards the end. It was Maisie's coughing fit. It bothered me – not because I was worried for her health (I'd stopped worrying about that), but because it had seemed unnatural somehow. Almost *put on*. Maisie may have been clever, but she wasn't a good actor, and that's what her interruption felt like: an act.

But why? What had we been talking about? I couldn't re-member. What had Donald been saying? Why should Maisie have wanted to shut him up like that? She could have just come straight out with it: she did with everything else! The whole thing made me uneasy, and yet I couldn't work it out.

At school, the big thing was Icarus. Nobody said anything, but Alan was still out to do someone in. I was Bed-ows now. Alex Bed-ows. And I didn't mind, not really. I'd always imagined that once you'd reacted, once everyone looked at you – gave you a name, they'd never stop looking. But they did. I suppose they got bored. Once I'd been labelled – the boy who couldn't get up in the morning – I could miss the bus as often as I liked. In a way, it was my Act Normal rule all over again: I wasn't acting normal for a normal person, but perfectly normal for Alex Stay-in-Bed-ows. As long as I wasn't linked with Bogsy – who was *weird* – it was OK.

We did have one thing in common, though, Bogsy and me. We both had this strange kind of freedom to go about our business unnoticed. How did Bogsy manage to get his notes and feathers in everyone's bags? Nobody saw because nobody looked. He was like the invisible man. (I made a point of not looking, these days, so as not to arouse his suspicions.) Bogsy's business was Icarus: setting the problem, conducting the teaser campaign. Mine was Icarus, too. Solving the problem, working everything out. Maisie's idea of telling a teacher was mad: I could do this myself.

I went to the shed again – Bogsy's, I mean – once Bogsy was safely on the bus.

It was still an awful mess. I twisted my ankle, treading on something buried under the rubbish: the plug to that big chest freezer they kept in there. Its prongs were sticking up and I couldn't help crying out in pain. Trust Bogsy to leave such a hazard lying around.

His sheet of maths homework had gone. In its place was a pile of familiar-looking slips of paper.

I counted them: twenty-eight. He was only doing our form, then: not the whole year, not the whole school.

And the message? Twenty-eight times over, I read one word: 'Sunset.'

There was something spooky about it. I didn't want to be there any more. It was only luck that I didn't step on the freezer plug again as I scrambled out. And I only just managed to make myself pause to shut the door behind me, before I ran.

The sunset notes weren't delivered that day. How could they be? Bogsy had left them behind when he went to school. Perhaps he'd just forgotten them, like he'd forgotten that sheet of maths.

All that day, I hugged myself. (Not literally, of course.) I had knowledge that nobody else had. I could have gone up to Alan like a fortune teller with a crystal ball, and said, *You will hear from Icarus tomorrow!* But I wouldn't have had time to say *what* he'd hear, before Alan screwed my head off.

So I did the pencil and paper thing, down in Don's shed. I drew a line down the middle of the piece of paper and wrote 'TIME' on one side and 'PLACE' on the other, these being the two bits of information Bogsy hadn't yet revealed. Which side of the line would sunset go?

I know the answer seems obvious, but I'd jumped to so many obvious conclusions since the Icarus thing began – and got them wrong. I didn't want to get caught out this time. Plus, I was reading a book at school called *Sunset is a Place*. In the book, Sunset House was the name of an old people's home. It was all a bit sad; one of the nicest old people died. That's what sunset made you think of: end-ings. 'The Laurels' was a much better name.

Under PLACE on my bit of paper I wrote 'Sunset Boulevard', which I'd heard of, and also 'Sunrise Court', which is part of the Sancton estate, down the road. If only it had been Sun*set* Court! Although, actually, I agreed with whoever had named it. Sunrise, being the start of the day, sounded hopeful. Sunset Court would have been a big downer, like Sunset House in the book.

After that, I couldn't think of any more places, and even the two I'd got were no good: Sunset Boulevard was in America and Sunrise Court didn't count. So I wrote 'Sunset (Icarus)' on the other side of the line.

Timmy got invitations from his friends that said, 'Please come to my party on Feb 19th at 2:15.' Parties were nice and 2:15 a reasonable time to have one.

But, 'Please come to watch me fly on Nov 2nd at sunset'?

That was *weird*. However you looked at it, even if you kept an open mind. I tried to keep mine open, but still it seemed wrong.

Things that flew didn't fly at sunset; at sunset they settled down for the night with their heads tucked under their wings. Icarus himself, in the story, had flown when the sun was high in the sky. At sunset, it wasn't just the sun that went down: so did everything else.

Everything? Birds (and boys) weren't the only things that flew. Soon it would be Halloween. Bats, witches, vampires flew, too – and *they* flew at night. They rose up when the sun went down. I imagined Bogsy lying on his back in that big chest freezer, like Dracula lying in his coffin. When darkness fell, the lid would creak open . . .

But that was stupid and only someone like Timmy would think like that. Someone like me knew that all you would find in a freezer was ice cream.

And then I remembered the upturned plug. At the time, I'd felt only annoyance with Bogsy, for leaving it there on the floor. Now, suddenly, it seemed very important.

There couldn't be any ice cream in Bogsy's freezer.

Bogsy's freezer wasn't plugged in.

So what *was* inside?

Not Bogsy: he went to school every day. Maybe

nothing. The freezer was probably empty and just being stored in the shed because there was nowhere else it could go.

Probably.

But I had to make sure.

Of course the pile of sunset notes had gone. They'd be on their way to school, hidden deep in Bogsy's bag. But, the next morning, everything else in Bogsy's shed looked the same. The same jumble of things was on top of the freezer: I'd have to move it all – carefully – before I could do what I'd come to do. And to put off doing that (because I felt nervous) I paused by the spy tube and looked through.

No Don – or Donald – today. The view I got was of part of the window, exactly the view I'd expected to get when I looked through before. The cobweb wasn't in the picture, though I knew it was there; just the dusty glass and daylight beyond. It seemed very homely on that side and suddenly very unsafe on this.

I moved to the freezer and picked up a slimy, brown apple core by its stalk. I put it on the floor beside another, more dried up, in a nest of crumpled old chewing gum wrappers. I put orange peel, two felt-tip pens, a key, a notebook (empty), some Sellotape and a lot of paint rags beside it. There was even a hiker's rucksack, removed from its frame. I put everything on the floor, except the chewing gum wrappers, which I stuffed in my pockets: I needed to keep them separate from the ones on the floor already, so I'd be able to put exactly the right amount back.

At last the surface was clear and I grasped the handle on the lid.

I'd been over so many things in my mind: what might happen, what I might find, when I lifted the lid. But I hadn't though of this. That the lid *wouldn't* lift. That no matter how much I pulled and shook and wiggled, it would not budge. But it wouldn't. And, in a funny way, I was relieved. I'd put everything back and catch the B17 and get given my sunset note, like everyone else. I'd still know – *un*like everyone else – who Icarus was. So it wasn't all bad.

Still, it was a shame. I checked the handle. There was

no release button, no catch that I'd missed. I ran my eye all round the seal – and there it was. Someone had screwed on a padlock fastening and then put a padlock on.

I bent to pick up the things from the floor that I'd have to put back. The apple core, the orange peel, the Sellotape, the pens. The first things I got hold of were the notebook and the key.

Not *the* key, of course, not the one for the padlock. That would be mad. No one would put on a padlock and then leave the key just lying around. I paused, with the key in my hand. I knew someone who might.

Breathing fast, I tried it in the lock.

Not just someone who might. Someone who had.

The clasp of the padlock sprang open and the lock plopped into my palm. I let it drop to the floor and took hold of the handle again and pulled upwards. And lifted the lid.

CHAPTER 13
WINGS

BANG!

I smashed the lid down again. Almost before I had seen inside. But I *had* seen. More than enough. I was shaking. Bogsy was mad. I refitted the padlock, quick.

Bogsy was mad to be keeping something like that shut up in there. *I* was mad to be getting anywhere near it. What was he *doing*? And, poking about in his business, what was I?

I'd better go to school and forget all about it.

But I knew I couldn't. Nobody could. Not after having caught sight of something like that.

I checked the padlock, to make sure I'd snapped it shut. The lid could burst open! But no, the lock was secure. It couldn't. Not even something like *that* could break out, no matter how much it thrashed about. And that's what it would be doing: thrashing about in terrible anger. Nothing less.

Because, imprisoned in Bogsy's freezer, there was a gigantic bird.

People say swans can break a man's arm. This bird was ten times the size of a swan! What if it had flown up in my face? What if it was an eagle or something, with talons? The plumage was rich and dark. But all I'd glimpsed was a wing.

The freezer stood silent again, keeping its secret. Hard to believe I'd seen what I'd seen.

But what *had* I seen? No actual thrashing about, no movement at all. Could the bird be dead? But no, there'd been no smell of death about it. (If anything, I realized, it had smelt ever so slightly of spearmint!) The feathers had gleamed, the greys, browns and blacks blending smoothly into each other, with the sleekness of health.

And yet perhaps not.

Here and there, there'd been a *thinness*. A bareness, like part of an old threadbare rug. Some of the quills of the feathers were showing in places. Maybe the bird was ill.

And now I was turning the key in the padlock again. I wasn't afraid any more. Softly, softly, I lifted the lid, and this time pushed it right up so it came to rest against the shed wall, amid Bogsy's suns.

The wing hadn't moved. And that's what it was, I realized now: not a bird, but a wing on its own. The wing of a bird, but not torn *from* a bird: made, put together, by someone.

When God made the world, people probably said to each other, How did he *do* it? As I gazed into Bogsy's freezer, all I could think was, *He* did *this*? Could the person who'd made all the mess and disorder around me also have made something stunningly neat? Yes, they could. Those shimmering suns on the wall should have told me: Bogsy was brilliant. He was an artist. This was his work.

When I was in Year 1 or Year 2, we'd made Native

American headdresses. Mrs Hill's husband worked on a farm, and she'd brought in loads of brown and black feathers. We each got a long strip of corrugated cardboard and Mrs Hill showed us how each little ridge was hollow and just the right size to hold the quill of a feather, if you poked one in. Auntie Jen sent me some of Squawky's, so mine had flashes of green, as well. It was ace. I brought it home at the end of term: that's when Dad had his first allergic reaction.

Maybe Bogsy knew someone who worked on that farm. But if so, he hadn't been satisfied. He'd gone out and got himself jays' feathers, doves' feathers, magpies' and starlings', too; down the leading edge of his wing, he'd even put swans' feathers – great curved white blades.

I felt like the man who first looked into Tutankhamun's tomb. When they asked him what he could see, all he managed to say was, 'Wonderful things.' The thing in the freezer was wonderful, too. I can't put it into any more words than that.

But it wasn't complete. There were those bare patches. What if Bogsy had run out of feathers? Run out before even starting wing number two? He must be making a pair, though I couldn't see anything underneath this one, and didn't dare lift it. What a shame if such an amazing project should fail for a stupid reason like that.

And that's when I had the idea. I thought it would make all the difference to Bogsy. (How could I know it would make all the difference to *me*?) Straight away, I was charging out of the shed, back through the wheelie bins, back up our garden; upstairs and into my bedroom – pushing my chair up against the wardrobe so I could reach the top, where Mum shoved the things she wasn't allowed to bin. (I could hear her now, with the radio on, preparing the room next door. She was folding up the sofa bed. I knew because she suddenly swore: the hinge had caught her finger.)

I fumbled about among the boxes and bags on top of the wardrobe. I had to do it by feel because it was too high up to see. I pulled at a bag that seemed promising but turned out to be the theatre I'd made from a shoebox in Year 5. Another was the overcomplicated board game Auntie Jen had given us last Christmas (and we'd never played). But here was one that felt more like it: a carrier bag, loosely tied at the handles. I opened it up and peered in.

I hadn't seen the headdress for years. The cardboard strip had been tightly rolled up and secured with a fat rubber band, so the feathers stood all in a bunch, like pens in a pen pot. I wasn't expecting that. But Squawky's green ones still showed up and it wasn't so bad. Quite convenient, really. I retied the bag, jumped down off the chair and hurried back out.

In Bogsy's shed I closed the freezer and put everything back how I'd found it, although there was no need to worry any more. To pretend that no one had been here was pointless now. The carrier bag was from Sainsbury's and bright orange: Bogsy would notice it straight away. I put it on top of the freezer, right in the middle, on top of everything else. I half wished I'd written a label: 'Please help yourself.' But there was no need. Or, 'From an Admirer', but then it wouldn't have been anonymous, would it? (Or would it? I get confused. Never mind.)

I didn't even mind the thought that my headdress

would be destroyed. It was going to be part of something much greater. And I would be part of it, too. That's what I wanted: not thanks, not praise, but just to know I'd contributed something. The work and the triumph would be Bogsy's, of course. And the flight – because obviously Bogsy was *going to fly*. (Maisie was wrong!) But, when he did, the flashes of green would be proof that I'd been involved.

That's all I wanted. The excitement of that remained, all the way to the bus stop. So did the faint smell of spearmint in my nostrils, which made it more real.

I found I had missed the first B17. I'd have to wait for the second. But any trouble I might get into at school was a small price to pay.

CHAPTER 14

DONALD

'Icarus and Alex Meadows!' said Mr Smith. 'What do they have in common?'

I stood uncomfortably in the doorway, longing to go to my place, but held where I was by Mr Smith's pointing finger. He was like Zeus, threatening me with a thunderbolt.

'They're both idiots!' shouted Alan Tydman.

'Wrong!' Mr Smith shouted back. 'Alex isn't an idiot, though he may behave like one.'

'Neither of them can get up in the morning?' shouted somebody else.

'Wrong again! Icarus got up *too high*! That's what caused his downfall. Alex hasn't had his downfall – yet. That's a clue, though. Come on!'

I looked at Bogsy. He was staring through the window at the sky. He had good reason to be interested in it – though perhaps he was only distancing himself from what was happening here in the room. I knew no more of his *character* than the rest of the class knew of mine – or, for that matter, any of us knew of Icarus's. Icarus was the boy who flew, Alex was the boy who stayed in bed. *We've both become known for one thing*, I could have suggested to Mr Smith.

'They're both boys ending in "s", sir!'

'Neither of them's got a "z" in their name!'

'All right! That's enough!' Mr Smith's pointing finger became an upturned Stop Where You Are sign. 'I'll tell you what Icarus and Alex have in common. They both pushed their luck. Alex, Miss McGowan has spoken to me –' Lydia and Candy went *Ooh*; he ignored them – '*Miss McGowan has spoken to me* about what's been going on – and it's got to stop. She's given you too many chances. I'm giving you *one*. This is it. Take one more, and you'll find yourself smashed –' he smacked his hand down on his desk – 'into tiny pieces, covered in a horrible, brown, sticky mixture of beeswax and blood! For all we know, there were nasty rocks in the Icarian Sea.'

Nobody laughed. I went and sat down. Bogsy was still looking out of the window, but of course he must have heard. I wondered what *he'd* used to fix his feathers in place: something better than beeswax.

I decided not to tell Maisie about the Native American headdress. I'd never kept something important from her before. But since she'd gone all funny about Icarus, I didn't trust her to react to things in the right way. She might say I shouldn't have done it – and leaving those feathers for Bogsy had been my master stroke. Besides, when I got to The Laurels on Saturday morning, she wasn't alone. Donald was there.

'G'day, Al!' he sang out cheerily. He didn't really have an Australian accent, but he could put one on. He was having a laugh. *Nobody* calls me Al and just for a moment I thought Alan Tydman had followed me in. I even glanced over my shoulder. But Donald didn't know Alan Tydman existed and, with luck, never would. It wasn't a good start, though.

'Hello,' I said, coldly.

Even without the headdress, there was so much news to tell Maisie: Bogsy's shed, his freezer, the wing, the sunset notes. Oddly, he still hadn't handed those out – and that was something I needed to discuss. But with Donald there, I couldn't say any of it. It was really annoying. 'You haven't gone back to Australia, then?' I asked rudely.

'Don't think so!' he said. He frisked himself quickly. 'Nope. Still here!'

'What's the matter?' said Maisie. 'Come in and sit down. Stop scowling. It doesn't suit you. Don't mind Donald. He knows everything. You can talk in front of him.'

'What d'you mean?'

'Donald knows what's been happening. With whasisname. I told him. You can talk to us both.'

'You *told* him?'

'Now, look here,' she snapped. 'What's wrong with that? For better, for worse, he's my boy and I trust him. *You* should tell one of your teachers. But I bet you haven't! Well, have you?'

There was no point carrying on if she wasn't on my side, and it seemed she wasn't. I needn't even answer her question, since it was one of those rhetorical ones Mr Smith talked about. She knew the answer already.

Lucky I'd never sat down. It made it easier to go. But just as I was about to, Donald said, 'Now, Ma, remember what *I* was like at Al's age. Don't be hard on him now. If he doesn't want to go to his teacher, why should he? It'll all be harmless fun. I'll eat my hat if it isn't!'

I looked at him, surprised. I hadn't thought *he* would stick up for me. I tried to imagine him wearing a hat: it would have to be one of those ones that Australians wear to keep the flies off, with corks hanging down all round the brim. The worst kind to eat!

But he wouldn't have to, would he? I was glad. And I made a decision.

'I've been to Icarus's place,' I said. 'I know what he's doing!'

Maisie just huffed but Donald said, 'You *do*?'

And so I told him. I told them both, only Maisie was sulking and wouldn't respond. I told them about Bogsy's shed, the mess (and the maths) and even the spy tube fixed to the wall. But I didn't mention Wonderland, since that was silly.

'You saw me, sitting in Dad's old shed?' said Donald. 'Well, I'll be . . .' He laughed. 'Good job I was behaving myself! D'you know, I spotted his bone-handle penknife and I *so* nearly took it! If I'd known I was under surveillance . . . Well, anyway, I didn't.'

'Didn't take it or didn't know?'

'Both. I only wanted a keepsake and I didn't think anyone would mind. But I'm glad to say I resisted the urge.' He held up his hands. 'Not guilty, M'lud!' He let them fall. 'So, what next? What else did you find?'

I told them about the freezer and the wing. They were impressed. Maisie tightened her lips to try to hide it, but Donald again said, 'Well, I'll be . . .' only with even more feeling now. 'He really *is* going to fly!'

Maisie couldn't contain herself at that. 'Boobies! *Both* of you!' she cried. 'Can't you see?' She snatched up her necklace and clasped it.

I ignored her. 'And I know when!'

I said about the sunset notes.

'Have you brought yours?' asked Donald in excitement. 'Come on! Where is it?'

I had to explain that for some reason Bogsy had still not handed them out. 'I think he forgot,' I added. 'He's quite absent-minded.'

Maisie gave up completely. 'Absent-minded? Not he!' she spluttered.

'He forgets to hand in his homework,' I pointed out.

'*Homework!* This one's got his mind on higher things than homework! Let's hope not too high – but don't say I didn't warn you!'

She let go of the necklace to raise both her hands in a gesture of hopelessness, then let them fall – flump – in her lap. She really was overreacting to this. There was an uncomfortable silence.

'Anyway, when *is* sunset?' I asked.

'When the sun sets,' she said, getting her own back.

'Ma!' said Donald. 'Don't tease. You know what Al means.'

He said he wasn't the best person to ask, since back

home (I thought Maisie winced at the word) it was summer. But, 'What d'you think, Ma? Six o'clock?' he mused. 'It gets earlier and earlier each day. Maybe half five?'

Maisie didn't answer, so I said, 'He's forgotten the notes, I just *know*! I'm going to remind him. I'm going to put a note in *his* bag . . .'

Maisie said nothing to that, but it got Donald going.

'No, no, you mustn't!' he said, alarmed. 'If he knows he's been rumbled, he may go to ground. Then we'll never find out what he's planning.'

How right I'd been to keep quiet about the Native American headdress! Feeling smug, I said innocently, 'Well, I've got to do *something*!'

'*Tell a teacher!*' said Maisie for about the hundredth time.

'Spoilsport!' said Donald, and they began to argue. She called him a booby and he returned with, 'Booby yourself!'

I said goodbye, but they barely noticed. Certainly nobody asked me to take a message home to Don.

At half past five that afternoon, I went to Don's shed. I wanted to watch the sunset and I wanted to find Don's penknife and I wanted to feel that Bogsy might be working away on his wings in the shed next door. Working and wondering who could have brought him his gift.

I wouldn't even mind if he took a look at me through his tube. I knew that artists did things their way. You just had to let them.

As for the setting sun, I was only surprised I had never noticed it before. I sat on my usual box and looked out at it. Perfectly framed in the doorway, it was. It was like a show put on especially for me. And it was amazing.

I don't think you're meant to stare at the sun. It makes you go blind or something. But I couldn't help it. (And I'm not blind yet.)

It was like a great, glowing apricot, only not any colour you could name. Not apricot colour, nor peach, nor orange; not pink and not red, not yellow and not even gold. When Bogsy was painting his suns on the wall, he must have wished they'd invent a new colour because none of the ones they'd invented already were right.

I tried to imagine him flapping along out there. How majestic he'd be! His wings would beat slowly; his body, I thought, would be carried underneath. (There's a type of bird that flies like that. I think it's a heron.) You might even hear a wheezing of air as you do when geese fly over. You wouldn't *see* anything in detail, only the black shape against the sun. You certainly wouldn't make out individual feathers, nor that, just here and there, some were green.

I looked around for Don's penknife and found it at last, in a pencil pot. It wasn't a pencil pot really, but a mug that had lost its handle and had a bunch of old pencils (and the knife) stuck in. The mug was dirty and chipped but still said clearly, 'World's Greatest Dad'.

I'd been wrong about Donald. I held the penknife in my hand and examined it closely. It was old but not rusty; not nearly as good as a Swiss Army knife, but OK. Although it had only two blades, its handle was lovely – the colour of honey and warmish to touch. I'd have liked to keep it.

But I wouldn't. I'd give it to him.

And then I got the idea that I'd put together a whole collection of keepsakes – things from the shed that he hadn't had time to look through before. He could take them back to Australia and remember the old days.

I put the knife in a biscuit tin, which already contained a mousetrap and a packet of parsley seeds. I added a small blue plate that said, in swirly writing, 'A present from Bournemouth'; also a little glass bottle of something called Tomorite. I pulled out a drawer from the old chest of drawers and balanced it over my knees so I could scrabble about for more things.

I wondered again if Bogsy was there. I was careful not even to glance towards the back wall. There was so much missing mortar, I couldn't have said which gap he looked through, even if I had wanted to, which I didn't. Let him look. That was fine by me.

Shadow was there, curled up, fast asleep, in an old, round washing up bowl. But the nibbler was silent, as it had been for weeks. I was glad. Mason bees were bad news. Since I'd got all excited about Icarus – found out so much and pushed things along – the idea of creatures that did so little made me twitchy. I put out a hand to stroke Shadow, and she curled up tighter for a moment.

I found another packet of seeds, but by now it was too dark inside the shed to make out what kind they were.

Too dark! I'd forgotten about the sunset. When I looked up, the whole sky was pink but the sun itself had dropped behind the trees so that only its top edge showed. It had certainly got a move on while I'd been looking in the drawer.

I checked my watch. I had to press the button to light up the display. 18:01. I checked the sky. Donald was right. Between half past five and six o'clock, the sun had set.

CHAPTER 15

PERSONAL

The sunset notes were delivered on Monday. Everyone had them by lunchtime and no one could talk about anything else. The girls enjoyed the spookiness of it: 'Ooh, it'll be getting *dark*!' The boys were tense because of Alan. Alan Tydman was in a rage.

Behind the science wall, he gave up trying to pretend he wasn't interested now.

Tom and Damien turned up with money, but Rob Bone sent them away.

'What time's sunset, then?' Alan jabbed his note back in its envelope and screwed the whole thing up in his fist.

'Six o'clock, Al,' I dared to say, 'or maybe before.'

'Bed-ows!' he snarled. 'Shut your gob! What do *you*

know?' He threw the screwed up paper in my face. I caught it and clutched it, as if that would help.

'Why can't he *say* six o'clock if he means it? What's his problem?' Alan went on.

But I was too scared to say any more. I could feel the ball of paper already moist from the sweat of my palm.

'What's *your* problem?' Suddenly Alan rounded on Rob Bone and Jack and the rest. 'What d'you think *you're* doing?' He swore and called them a load of insulting names.

Someone was going to get hurt, for sure. It was going to be soon. It was going to be bad. Pointless to try and guess who it would be. It would be whoever was unlucky enough to be nearest when Alan lost control. In a way, he already had. That's what this was about. He commanded his Battalion: gave us our ranks, our places, our orders. That was the way it was meant to be and we knew where we were. Alan commanded Alan's Battalion, but he wasn't directing the Icarus Show.

And he wouldn't be able to tolerate it much longer.

But nothing happened that lunchtime because the bell

went before it could. Silently and gratefully, we left the wall and went in.

For old time's sake, I took my envelope down to Don's shed. I hadn't opened it at school because I didn't need to. I almost didn't open it now, but I liked the idea of repeating patterns. The spider was there. Maybe Bogsy was, too, peering down his tube. I hoped he was: I thought I could put on a little show of my own.

I wiggled my finger under the flap and broke the seal. There was the slip of white paper inside. I brought it out with a tiny flourish and held it up to read.

Nothing.

I turned it over.

Still nothing.

The paper was blank on both sides. I felt confused.

My first thought was, Has he gone to ground? Donald had said he might. Foxes did, when the hounds got too close. The nibbler had, when summer was over.

A person would go to ground if they felt a pursuer hot on their heels. Had Bogsy felt me hot on his? How had he guessed who the feathers were from? And anyway, they were a present – something nice, something useful, not *threatening* at all.

No, he had not gone to ground. He'd given out notes to everyone else, hadn't he? This was personal. You wouldn't have thought it could be: a blank piece of paper in a blank envelope. But in fact I'd never received such a personal thing in all my life. 'You!' it screamed. 'You! *You!* YOU!' In the silence, I put my hands up to my ears, it seemed so loud.

Did it cross my mind that there'd been some mistake? Yes, it did, but I knew that there hadn't been. Bogsy might be forgetful, but this was deliberate, a thought-out thing. It was a response.

And then I was angry.

I'd given Bogsy a present. And somehow he'd worked out who I was – and done this. He'd pushed me away, cut me out of the circle, given me – made me – even less than the others. I deserved more!

And then I lost control, but not in an Alan Tydman way. I mean my brain wasn't in control of what I did next.

I sprang from my box and ran out of the shed. I pulled the wheelie bins apart and burst through. Then I was outside Bogsy's shed and, without hesitation, opening the door. Before I could properly see inside (but I *knew* he was there), 'Where's my note?' I exploded. 'My sunset note? I should get one, like everyone else!'

He was sitting in his chair, which was the sort they have in offices – grey, with cushiony bits and a swivel device. He was sitting up straight, with his arms on the armrests. He looked like a king on a throne, waiting for one of his subjects to appear. It was disconcerting, but I stood my ground. He'd been expecting me.

The only bit of him that moved was his jaw. He was chewing something large and resistant. The little muscles behind his eyes were working like mad. But when I repeated, 'Where's my sunset note?' he said nothing.

I was very aware that beside him, laid out on the freezer, was the wing. I wanted to look and see if he'd added in any of my green feathers, but his eyes were challenging me to look, so I didn't. I was angry and wasn't going to be pushed around.

I was going to ask how he'd worked out the gift was from me. I'd demand to know. I'd no idea where this would end, but that seemed a good enough place to start.

I never even got that far.

To show I wasn't interested in what was lying on the freezer, I very deliberately looked away. I looked down at the floor. And there was the answer.

On the floor, in amongst all the rubbish, was the head-dress, now unrolled. He hadn't removed any feathers; he hadn't even cared that they might get damaged. The card-board strip had flopped open (except where it still curled a bit at the ends) and the back – the bit that's not meant to show – was uppermost. There, halfway along, in Mrs Hill's super-big, super-clear Key Stage 1 writing, was 'Alex Meadows' in chunky red marker pen.

I wanted to fall through a hole in the floor, and vanish like Rumpelstiltskin. Not that I was angry now. Just *embarrassed*. I'd so nearly asked how he knew it was me! It was only luck that I hadn't.

What if I had? It was cold in the shed, but my face

burned hot at the thought. I waited for him to call me stupid and tell me to get out.

But he didn't. Instead he said, 'What d'you want?'

That took me by surprise. That was what you might say to someone who'd backed you into a corner. *I'll give you what you want, if you'll let me go.*

I'd definitely not cornered Bogsy! Far from it. I'd shown myself up.

And then: but had I? What did it look like to *him*? I'd discovered his secret! I'd delivered him a package, much as he'd been delivering Icarus notes. Only I'd put my real name on mine – which was bold! He wasn't to know I'd not meant to.

'You g—' He started to speak, but found he couldn't because of the thing in his mouth. He took it out – a ball of chewing gum almost the size of an egg – and sat it in a jam tart case on the table. Then he started again.

'You gonna mess things up?'

'No!'

'Then what d'you want?'

What did I?

The things I had wanted five minutes ago weren't relevant now.

'I want . . .' I began. 'That is, I'd like, to . . . help.'

I sounded like a little kid asking to help an adult make a cake – right after they've spilled the bag of raisins on the floor.

Bogsy didn't answer. I thought he was going to put the chewing gum back, but instead he took two little slips of paper from the table. Then his arms were resting on the chair's arms again, and one of the slips was in one hand, one in the other. The one in his right hand was a sunset note, I saw. I couldn't read what (if anything) was written on the one in his left.

He looked at me hard, narrowing his eyes, as if I were a sum he had to get right. Then, 'Give us that,' he said, and nodded towards *my* right hand. I hadn't realized I was still holding the envelope with its blank slip inside. I stepped forward and dropped it in his lap.

Still looking at me in that calculating way, and still holding *his* two slips of paper, he tweaked out the blank one from the envelope and flicked it aside. It was all so weird. By now I'd have been content to get given my sunset note, and go. Just to forget it.

But eventually he put in the slip from his left hand and gave the envelope back. Then he replaced his huge lump of gum and swivelled his chair round to face away.

'Bye, then,' I said to the back of his head. It was clear the discussion was over. I didn't expect an answer and didn't get one. He was chewing again.

In Don's shed, I opened my envelope for the second time that day. The slip of paper inside was not blank now.

'Same time. Same place. Tomorrow,' it said.

Bogsy was giving me the benefit of the doubt.

CHAPTER 16
CONSTRUCTION WORK

'Yeah?' came Bogsy's voice when I knocked on his shed door after school next day. We had walked home separately from the bus stop, but almost at once I'd come round, as the note had said.

I felt guilty, waiting for permission to enter, as if I'd never been in all those times unasked; as if yesterday had never happened, when I'd rudely burst in without knocking.

Inside, it was worse. Bogsy had the wing laid out on top of the freezer again.

For a moment, I was tempted to pretend I'd never seen it. I could express surprise and amazement, go up close and examine the workmanship as if for the very first time.

But Bogsy would know. He would know I was lying, and everything would be spoilt.

So I just said, 'It's great, that,' and hoped he would understand why I couldn't say more.

If he did, he didn't show it. 'Gum,' he said, and held out a piece without looking up. He was bending over the wing, doing something delicate with his right hand, fingers spread.

'No, thanks,' I said, but I thought it was nice he'd asked.

'Then why've you come?'

That was really confusing. Not to chew gum, I wanted to say, but that would have made things worse. 'To help?' I offered.

He flashed me a glance. 'Oh, not to spy, then?'

That was really *unfair*. I felt it so strongly, I said so. 'Unfair!' I exclaimed. '*You* spied on *me*!' I glanced at the tube sticking out of the wall. 'Why did you?'

Bogsy straightened up and again looked towards me for a second. He seemed uncomfortable, which he never had before. 'Dunno,' he said. And then he was angry. 'It

141

was *stupid*!' He stepped towards the tube and dashed it away. I couldn't tell if he was angry because he had lowered himself to spying or because he had done something for *no reason*. It could have been either of these – or both. The cardboard tube lay wrecked on the floor, but somehow his outburst had cleared the air.

'Here,' he said. 'Go on.'

He must have forgotten I'd said no thanks to the gum, because he was holding out a piece to me again. What was wrong with him? But this time I took it.

'Over here,' he said.

We both moved across to the wing. He was chewing, himself, I saw now, though not as much gum as he'd had in his mouth yesterday. He took a small brown feather from a box (it was over half full; I needn't have worried) and chose a place on the wing where coverage was thin. He tucked the feather beside another, carefully patting and smoothing it down till it seemed to belong. Its quill rested on a crosspiece, which looked like a spoke from an umbrella.

And then, all at once, the mystery was solved. (Or this

one, anyway.) It happened so quickly, I wouldn't have seen if I'd even just glanced away. He licked his finger and thumb and pinched out a small bit of gum from his mouth and pressed it on top, welding quill and crosspiece together.

Bogsy's beeswax!

I popped my own piece of gum in my mouth, and started to chew.

'Why d'you use spearmint?' I asked.

'Cos I like it.' He looked surprised at the question. 'Least I used to. I'm sick of it now.'

'You could try a different flavour?' I said, but all he replied was, 'My *jaw* aches,' and there seemed no answer to that. To fill the awkward silence, I said, 'Well, you have to chew it!'

'Not any more, I don't,' but he didn't say why not.

It was really difficult, talking, and not just because we were chewing at the same time. The conversation kept going off in strange directions, or petering out. So I was relieved when he started explaining how to remove a piece of gum from my mouth without getting stuck to it. ('Lick your fingers first.') He seemed very concerned that I learn the technique. Which was thoughtful of him.

'You're going to have to work fast,' he said. 'You've got to be able to do it.'

I licked my finger and thumb, just as he had, and pinched out a piece of gum from the lump in my mouth. I took about half. Then I scanned the wing for a bare patch and reached out my hand.

WHAM!

Bogsy shot *his* hand out and hit mine away. He made me jump and I dropped the gum. It seemed an overreaction, but I thought he'd done it because I'd forgotten to take a feather first. 'Oh, sorry . . .' I began.

But, 'You're not touching *that*!' he said fiercely. He meant the wing.

'Then, how . . . ?'

'Only *I* get to work on that.'

'But you said . . .'

'You chew.'

It turned out my job was just to chew gum. So he wouldn't have to. I'd be like one of those dogs in medieval times that ran round a treadmill while somebody else did the interesting stuff.

'Take it or leave it,' said Bogsy, and I knew if I left it, I'd leave the shed and never come back.

It was a no-brainer.

I licked my finger and thumb once again and took out the small piece of gum that was still in my mouth. Bogsy watched me in silence. Then I gave it to him.

He licked his own finger and thumb and took it. He didn't say thanks. But neither did he whack me again.

So I knew we had an agreement.

After that, we worked together, me chewing, him choosing and sticking on feathers. I admired his skill, but we worked without talking: I *couldn't* say much because of the gum; he didn't want to. I tried to keep two or three pieces on the go in my mouth at any one time. That way, no matter how quickly he went, I was able to keep him supplied. I'd have liked to remind him about my head-dress, which was still in a heap on the floor. But maybe, at that stage, I wouldn't have, even without my mouthful of gum. I had loads of questions, but didn't ask one. One *was* answered in the end, but not by me asking, only by chance.

'David!' somebody called (it was Bogsy's mum) when we'd been there a while. At first he didn't react, just went on working, so I did, too. But when she called again, his hand stopped mid-way to the box of feathers.

'David! Tea!'

He closed the box and shoved it away. Then he started, ever so gently, gathering up the wing in his arms.

I don't know how he managed to get it in and out of the freezer on his own. On this occasion, I was allowed to lift the lid. And so, just before he slid the wing inside, I saw what I hadn't before. Lying at the bottom – yes – another. Its pair.

But totally different. No feathers on this one, just a wing-shaped construction of criss-crossing spokes and canes. It was more like a *diagram* of a wing and – maybe because it was complicated – it made me think of maths. I didn't know if Bogsy would mind that I'd seen, but I couldn't help bursting out, 'Wow! Look at *that*!'

And all he said was, 'Got to put feathers on that one.'

'I could help you!' I said, excited. 'We could do it together, over half-term.' Half-term was next week. 'I'm not going away! Are you?' He frowned and looked at the floor. 'I could come every day and – chew!'

He didn't say yes, but he didn't say no. So I said, 'See you tomorrow.' I didn't mean at school. '*Same time, same place!*'

As I slipped through the bins and ran back up our garden, all I could think was how brilliantly things had turned out. Bogsy would fly *with my help*: in his wings would be tell-tale flashes of green (I'd make sure). It was good to be in on the secret, good to be sharing something with someone at last. Even someone so strange.

Mr Smith had explained to us how things in books could symbolize things. Perhaps they could in real life. As Bogsy and I worked away on his wonderful wings, perhaps we were building something else, too.

CHAPTER 17
CHANGES

Bogsy *hated* Alan's Battalion. He hated them for being a gang and for having power over everyone else, although individually, as he said, they were just a bunch of morons.

And the bad news was, he thought I was one of them.

'You what?' I said.

'You hang out with them, don't you?'

And I realized that's what it looked like from the outside.

'So what am I doing now?' I said.

Hanging out with *him*, that's what. (Something I never thought I'd do.)

But Bogsy shrugged. 'How should I know?'

You gonna mess things up? he had asked on Monday.

That seemed years ago. So much had happened since then, so much had changed.

Today, for example, Friday, he'd been using feathers from my headdress. I'd finally plucked up the courage to suggest it, and he hadn't said no.

'Use some of Squawky's – the green ones,' I said. 'They'd be good.'

'Squawky's?' said Bogsy. 'Who's *Squawky*?!'

And suddenly he was laughing. I'd never seen him laugh (and I didn't again, not for ages). At first I thought he had hiccups, but when he got going I understood. When he got going, he *let himself go*. He flailed his arms and knocked over a box: loads of feathers came out and he grabbed great handfuls and threw them recklessly into the air.

'Squawky . . .' I tried to explain, but as soon as I said the name again, I realized how funny it was and had to take out my gum, in case I choked. I didn't have time to lick my fingers first, though: the gum got stuck to them, and I was jumping around, getting stuck to things and laughing with Bogsy.

And when it was over, the air in the shed felt different. Bogsy went back to the wing and stuck a green feather beside a pure black one. It looked great. I took a deep breath.

'Do you think . . .' I began. 'Do you think, when we've finished . . . I mean finished them both . . . Well, d'you think I could just have a go?'

Bogsy was scrabbling round on the floor, stuffing feathers back in the overturned box, making quite a bit of noise. I *thought* he said, 'Only Icarus dies,' but I must have misheard.

'Daedalus flies as well,' I said. 'Don't forget that. The two of them do.'

'Daedalus was his *dad*!' Bogsy flashed. 'You're not my dad!'

The suddenness of his anger took me aback.

'What's the plan, then?' I said. But it was too late.

So much had changed in the shed that week, but Bogsy still didn't trust me. He was letting me help – and we'd just had a laugh – but still there were things he was keeping to himself.

'I've made friends with him!' I announced when I went to The Laurels the following day. Maisie was in her chair and Donald was perched on the bed, eating biscuits.

They knew who I meant and Maisie said, 'At last!'

Donald said, 'What happened? How did you do it?' and I said, 'Well, he gave out the sunset notes and I went round and told him I knew it was him and we talked. No sweat.'

'Was he surprised?' asked Donald excitedly. 'What did he say?'

'Not much. He never does. But we get along fine.'

The way I described it, it sounded so simple, so normal, so everyday.

'I'll be going round his a lot next week. You know, because it's half-term.'

'Has he said why he's doing it?' asked Donald, but Maisie cut in before I could say any more.

'Never mind why he's doing it. Alex, you'll be able to stop him now.'

'Stop him?' I said. 'What d'you mean? I'm *helping* him. Next week we're getting the second wing done. Why would I want to stop him? He's going to *fly*!'

Why couldn't she see?

'Then I'll go to him myself,' she said stubbornly. 'You must arrange it.'

'So you can stop him?' I wasn't that stupid.

'No.'

'But you said . . .'

'*I* couldn't stop him. No. What I want is to meet him and see if I'm right. You must fix up a visit. And you –' she pointed to Donald – 'will drive me.'

If she saw the wings, she would see she was wrong. I suddenly wanted her to. Who, when they saw them, wouldn't want Bogsy to fly?

'Someone's been trampling my pumpkin plants,' said Mum. 'Down by Don's shed.' She looked at me. She knew it was me, not because she'd seen me, but because I was the only person who went down there.

When I visited Bogsy next day, I made sure she was on

the phone to a patient, well out of the way. But I was worried. I told Bogsy.

'I can't come through the wheelie bins any more,' I said. 'My mum's on my back about treading on her plants. If she catches me at it, she'll want to know where I'm going, and then we'll be stuffed.'

'Come through the house,' said Bogsy straight away.

Partly, I was relieved: I'd feared he might say, Stop coming, then, why don't you?

But, 'What d'you mean, come through the house?' I said. 'How – when I don't even live in it now?'

'Well,' he said, speaking slowly. (I had that feeling again that I was a child and he was much older.) 'You open the gate, walk up the path and ring the bell.' He was being sarcastic, but I didn't mind.

I liked the idea of visiting as he described. I liked its ordinariness. I'd had enough of climbing through the wall of wheelie bins. And it would be public. People would see me. Not so much now, but after half-term, Alan Tydman would. And that would be fine. It would prove I'd changed.

And then I realized that using the door instead of the bins had another advantage.

'Can I bring a friend?'

He stiffened at once.

So I added, 'Not from school.'

'Not Alan Tinybrain?'

'No! A *friend*! You'd like her.'

'A girl?'

'No, she's old. An old lady.'

He looked at me questioningly.

'She's – wise.' Yes, that was the word. 'And she wants to come.'

'You told? About this?' He suddenly slammed his palm down on the table; a couple of loose feathers jumped off the edge. Then he turned away.

'I trust her!' I said. It was like an echo of something someone had said before. 'I'd never tell people at school, but Maisie's different. She used to live here before we moved, before you came. Now she lives in a Home.' I paused. 'She never gets out, but she used to. *Before you came.*'

It sounded like I was accusing him. Like it was all his fault, about Maisie. It wasn't, of course, but I'd had enough. I would say what I liked.

'Maisie's unusual.' His back was still turned, so I carried right on. 'Like you.'

He spun round. 'What d'you mean?'

There was no going back.

'She doesn't see things in the same way as other people. Her world is different. I think you'd – get on.'

I thought he was going to laugh or be angry, but he showed no emotion at all when he looked me straight in the eye and said, 'No.'

CHAPTER 18

MEETING OF MINDS

I am a cautious person. Don't know if you've noticed. Timmy takes risks (and they often work out) but I don't. I like to play safe. As we walked up the path to Bogsy's front door (which used to be mine) and rang the bell, it didn't feel safe at all.

Safety in numbers, they say. There were three of us waiting on Bogsy's doorstep, me and two others, but that was the point: I'd taken a massive risk, bringing them here.

Being in a Home must have weakened Maisie's legs. She needed help getting out of the car; she needed support to walk from there to the house. By the time we reached the gate, we'd arranged it so Donald and I were on either side and Maisie could hold Donald's arm with one hand and clutch my shoulder (I wasn't as tall as Donald) with the other. The path was barely wide enough for the three of us, but we managed. We must have looked pretty extraordinary, though, and this was reflected in Bogsy's mum's expression when she opened the door.

'Oh!' Then she focused on me. 'Oh, Alex! It is Alex, isn't it? Yes, of course. How nice. I've been saying for ages how nice it would be if . . . But who . . . ? Why . . . ?' She stopped in confusion. That was OK. Even if I'd told Bogsy, Bogsy probably wouldn't have told her. Maisie and Donald would guess that was it.

'Sorry to bother you,' said Donald. 'I'm Donald Brett. I grew up next door.' He held out his hand and almost caused Maisie to fall over. She tightened her grip on my shoulder and took charge.

'What my son's trying to say is we won't inconvenience you. We've come to see David.'

I'd never used his name with her. It was clever of her to know it – and use it now. But his mum looked frightened.

'Oh, dear, has he done something? What? I'm so sorry. I knew things were . . . But . . . I'm so *sorry* . . .'

'No, *no*!' said Maisie. 'He's done nothing wrong. They've been working on something together, he and Alex, down in the shed. You'll know about that. It's nearly finished. They've invited me here for a private view.'

I almost wished Bogsy's mum would object. No, sorry, I can't allow this. But of course she didn't. She didn't stand a chance against Maisie's determination. Poor Mrs Marsh.

'Oh, but I didn't . . .' She didn't know anything. Not about Maisie, not about Donald, not about Bogsy down in the shed. 'You'll come in for a cup of tea first?'

'I will not,' said Maisie. 'If you don't mind, I'll go straight through.' We were moving forward as she spoke.

'You'll sit down for a minute?' said Mrs Marsh helplessly.

'Alex, is there a chair in the shed?' Maisie asked.

I said there was.

'I'll sit there, then,' she said, and we kept on going.

I was surprised how little they'd changed things. All their furniture was in, of course, but the carpets and

wallpaper – even the curtains – were ours. Then I remembered Don's shed, with all Don's stuff all over the place
and Mum and Dad's stuff shoved into a corner. Don's
shed was still Don's. (That's why I liked it.) Perhaps it
wasn't so surprising that Bogsy's family hadn't redeco-
rated. Things take time to change.

There didn't seem to be anyone around. Bogsy didn't
have brothers or sisters – or cats or dogs – but he'd got a
dad, I knew. I'd seen his dad carrying boxes into the
house, the day they moved. I'd noticed him especially
because he'd looked unusually tall. I wondered what his
job was. Whatever it was, it must be where he was now.

Then, as we stepped outside the back door, Mrs Marsh
shouted, 'Mind the sand!'

A massive mountain of sand was blocking our way and
our view down the garden. We stopped in time, of course,
and went round it, but I was shocked. What would you
want with a massive mountain of sand?

Mrs Marsh didn't come round the mountain. She
stayed in the house. Maisie and Donald and I went on
alone.

When I knocked on the door of the shed, Bogsy said, 'Yeah,' as he always did. And, as always, I turned the handle. Maisie and Donald peered in. Maybe one of them said something, I'm not sure. I'm not sure what it was that alerted Bogsy to the fact that something was wrong. But he looked up.

For a moment, he looked like a creature surprised in its lair. A fox run to earth. Then he sprang to the door and grabbed it and banged it shut.

That was it.

Donald said, 'Oh.'

I didn't dare look at either of them. Now they knew.

There was no invitation.

I'd been trying my luck, and my luck had run out.

But Maisie stepped forward and rapped on the door with her sharp, bony knuckles.

'David!' she said. 'Open up at once! Do you hear?'

Silence.

'Open this door!'

'Go away.'

'David, you *must* open up. I'm old and tired. *I have to sit down.*'

She made it sound like something awful would happen if she didn't. Perhaps it would. We never found out because Bogsy opened the door.

Maisie let go of Donald and me and made a break for inside. She surged past Bogsy and sank down into his chair. She was breathing hard. Donald and I stepped in, too, so there we all were. '*Now!*' Maisie said.

I couldn't look at any of them. So I looked at the wing, which was out on top of the freezer – yes, pretty much finished. I waited for them to start shouting at me. I waited years. But they didn't. So I looked up. There was something strange going on.

Bogsy was staring at Maisie. Maisie was sitting in Bogsy's chair with her arms on the armrests, just like him. Bogsy was staring at her as he'd once stared at me. I felt sorry for her. But when I looked into her face, I saw it was fine: she was staring back!

Maisie was sizing *him* up! Working *him* out! You wouldn't have thought two people so different – a boy and a frail old woman – could be so alike. Yet I'd been right. They were more than alike. They were kind of the same.

Then Donald caught sight of the wing – 'Gee!' he said – and the spell was broken. 'That's *fantastic*! Look, Ma!'

But she wouldn't.

She knew it was there, but she would not look. 'He's a clever young man,' she said. That was all.

Another Greek myth we'd done at school was Medusa, who, if you looked at her, turned you to stone. Maisie not looking was like a person protecting themselves. I was so disappointed. I'd brought her to look (not be turned to stone, of course, just impressed). But she was too clever. She raised her hand to her necklace in the old familiar way.

And Bogsy said sharply, 'What's that?' He was peering intently at the necklace, stretching his own neck out to see.

Rats' teeth and razor blades.

His kind of thing. He could ask where she'd got it and get one himself.

But she didn't say what I'd expected.

'I made it.' She watched his expression. 'When I was a girl. About your age.'

Well, I never guessed *that*!

I could not imagine Maisie as a girl. I could not imagine her making the pendant.

But perhaps Bogsy could. Because now it was he who said something surprising.

'Here. Put this on, if you like.'

His expression hadn't changed, but he was offering her a feather.

I couldn't believe it! He'd not allowed *me* to do anything other than chew.

But she wouldn't take it.

'No,' she said and then, oddly, 'I don't agree.'

Bogsy shrugged like he couldn't care less.

'Have it your way,' he said. 'I'm still gonna fly.'

It was like the end of an argument they'd had, but no words had been spoken. They'd met for the first time two minutes ago and yet they were acting as if they'd been talking for hours.

'Silly boy!' exclaimed Maisie. Which got him going, good and proper.

'Silly? You calling me silly?'

'I am.'

'Well, what about *them*? Everyone else?'

'What about them?'

'D'you know what it's like when everyone's *stupid*? There's no one to talk to!'

'And you think the solution is . . .'

'Fly away. Yeah. Too right!'

Then Maisie was angry. 'No! *Not* right: wrong! If you can't see that, you're more stupid than them!'

None of it made any sense – and then it got worse.

In a quieter voice, Maisie went on: 'But there was someone, wasn't there? Someone who proved they were not quite so stupid . . .'

Who? I wondered.

'Somebody clever enough –' said Maisie, who seemed to be able to read my thoughts – 'someone clever enough to work out who Icarus was.'

I stared at her then. Then I stared at him. Then I stared

at the light streaming in through the shed's one window.

'So you can't say everyone's stupid, can you? You can't say you're all alone any more!'

Bogsy laughed, but not in the way a person would laugh if their problems were over.

I knew why.

He was puzzled. There was something he couldn't work out.

And that something was me.

I looked at Maisie. She knew. What if she told him? Told him I'd got the answer not by cleverness but by chance?

What if he asked?

I remembered seeing my name in great big letters along the cardboard strip of the Native American headdress. I was as stupid as anyone else! *More* stupid. Bogsy suspected as much, but the evidence was confusing.

He only need ask.

But then Maisie changed tack. 'Anyway, cleverness isn't the be-all and end-all, you know. If you've not found a genius, just be grateful you've found a . . . somebody who'll stand by you. Anyone's lucky if they've got that.'

I thought she meant Donald, standing by her. Donald had gone to Australia and come back. She might have meant Donald, but she was looking at Bogsy. Bogsy and me.

The two of them, Bogsy and her, had been talking as if me and Donald weren't there. *I* didn't mind, I was happy to listen (or, more like, I was stunned), but Donald was different. He'd had enough.

'So, Dave,' he said suddenly, 'how long did all this take? How many feathers? Where did you get them?'

By the time Maisie said she wanted to go, Bogsy was looking like *he'd* had enough. When Donald asked what kind of glue he'd used, I said, 'Beeswax!' as a joke, and to shut Donald up.

'Come again,' Bogsy said to Maisie. Which was the last thing you'd think he'd have said.

But Maisie said, 'No, I won't come again.'

He was about to say something more, but she interrupted. 'You don't need *me*. You think you do, but you don't. You're going to be fine.'

Again he began to object, and again she went on.

'You're *lucky*,' she said. 'Think about it.'

I don't know whether he did or not. But when Donald took one last look at the wing and spotted a green feather near the top and asked where it had come from, Bogsy said something under his breath: I think, that he'd got it from a friend.

CHAPTER 19
THE MOUNTAIN

He never did ask how I'd worked out who Icarus was. (And he never realized my name on the cardboard strip had been a mistake.) I think he was way too proud to admit there was something he couldn't understand. He was a very proud person. I learned that.

Then again, perhaps Maisie's words had sunk in and he just didn't want to know. Either way, he seemed more relaxed with me, less suspicious.

Maisie and Donald had come on Monday. Now the half-term week stretched ahead, free from school, free from Alan's Battalion. It turned out to be the best week I'd had since starting at Lambourn.

We finished the first wing and moved to the second.

Wing number two. Bogsy began at the tip (not the top), which wasn't what I'd have expected – but I could see why. That way, each new row of feathers naturally overlapped the ones he'd already put on. He'd worked it all out.

And we talked about stuff, as we worked. On Tuesday, Bogsy suddenly said, 'How old is she?'

Because he so rarely asked questions, I was taken aback. Of course I knew who he meant. But this was a good excuse to take out my gum (my jaw ached constantly now) and I wanted to make the most of it. So I said, 'Who?'

He shot out a hand and deliberately knocked mine back against my chest. Which meant the gum got stuck to my jumper.

'Get off!' I said, pulling it free. It was covered in fluff. 'Maisie, d'you mean? I don't know.'

'I reckon she's *old*. She could die.'

'Don't be stupid!'

'What happened to her husband?'

'He . . .' I stopped. I had no alternative: quickly I made a lunge with the gum, trying to stick it on *him*. He dodged,

169

lost his balance and fell over. But as he went, he grabbed my leg. And then we were skirmishing on the floor, amongst all the rubbish. It was great.

I was trying to stuff chewing gum wrappers and dried up orange peel in his mouth. I don't know what he was trying to do, but as we were both as useless as each other, it was fine. We carried on till we heard a knock on the door.

Bogsy's mum made it her business to bring us biscuits and squash all the time, but she always knocked first and we always had time to slide the wing back in the freezer. We quickly got up and slid it back now, and then Bogsy opened the door.

'What *have* you been doing, David?' He was gasping for breath and there was stuff in his hair.

'Fighting!' he said.

'Oh *dear*!'

'Don't worry, just messing about,' I put in.

'Thank goodness!'

She liked me, I knew. Bogsy said she'd never brought biscuits to the shed before I came.

When she'd gone, and we'd downed the squash, I said, 'Why's your dad never here? What's he do? What's his job?'

'He's in the construction industry,' Bogsy said grandly.

I waited. 'And?'

'He's a brickie. Builders get him to build walls.'

'Oh.' Why didn't they build their own walls? What *did* they do? I thought about asking. I thought about Daedalus, Icarus's dad, who built the Labyrinth – and I asked something else.

'What's your dad's name?'

He gave me a funny look. 'Colin.' Then he went on.

'I was going to be a brickie,' he said. 'When I grew up. Like Dad. I was Dad's apprentice. I was good.'

I waited again. 'So what happened?'

'Lambourn,' he said shortly.

As an answer, it didn't really work. I mean, I could understand that Lambourn had spoiled things – it had for me – but not *everything*. When you go to Lambourn, the non-Lambourn things become *more* important. Not less.

'Yeah,' I said. 'I know. But why give up building with

your dad? I don't get it.' Alan Tydman could wreck your life between half past eight and five past three, but not all of it. Why chuck the rest of it away?

Bogsy fiddled with the handle of the freezer. We hadn't got the wing back out. He started lifting the lid, as if to now, then shut it again.

'Dad left,' he said. 'He gave up on me.'

'Oh.'

'At the start of term. He went. He didn't come back.'

I thought of the mountain of sand outside their back door. When people leave, they don't *just* leave, they leave problems to be got round.

CHAPTER 20
SHEDS

'Oh, there you are, Alex,' said Mum, as soon as I walked in through the back door. 'We've been looking for you. I suppose you were down in the shed?'

'Which shed?'

'Don't be silly.'

'I'm not. I *was* in a shed, actually, but not ours.'

'Oh! Next door, were you? With your friend? David, is it?'

'Why were you looking for me?' I asked crossly.

'We're all going to Lampwick's for lunch. For a treat. You need to get ready.'

Dad had taken time off work, to be with his family over half-term – and their idea of a great day out was to go to a garden centre!

Mum coughed. 'Why don't you see if David would like to come, too?'

They'd never met Bogsy, but I knew they were pleased I'd been going round his such a lot. I knew Mum's casualness was fake. It was really annoying.

'He wouldn't want to come,' I said rudely. '*I* don't want to come! You can leave me here.'

Dad walked in, looking smug. 'It's not what you think,' he said meaningfully and raised his eyebrows. 'Your mum and I have got something important to tell you. When we get there. Your friend might be interested in it, as well.'

'He wouldn't,' I said.

'Oh, don't be silly, Alex,' said Mum for the second time in two minutes. 'You don't even know what we're going to say. If *you* won't invite him, I'll do it myself . . .' She reached for her coat.

'No!' I said very loudly. 'I'll ask him, OK?'

'Lunch?' said Bogsy. 'In Lampwick's? Why?'

'It's their idea of fun.'

His mouth twitched. He was trying not to smile.

'They've got some big announcement to make. A surprise.'

'Nice or nasty?' He was serious now.

'Not nasty,' I said, 'or they wouldn't want you to be there. It's probably boring.' I wanted to get him to say he didn't want to come and then I could tell Mum and Dad that I'd tried, and that would be that. But he didn't. He said he'd once had a toastie in Lampwick's and he wouldn't mind one again. He went to the house to tell his mum he'd be out for lunch.

Timmy loved Lampwick's. He loved it because of the sheds. That was funny because at home he took no interest in Don's shed at all, and he hadn't been interested in our other shed, either – before we moved. But maybe it wasn't so funny. The sheds at Lampwick's were something else.

At Lampwick's, yes, there were tool sheds and potting sheds, storage sheds and mower sheds and sheds to keep your bikes in. But also there were summerhouses – play-houses and Wendy houses – even a gingerbread house, painted with giant jelly diamonds for roof tiles and rows of giant sponge fingers for walls.

I used to like all that, too. When I was little – and Timmy was littler – we'd always beg Mum and Dad to go to the shed section first of all. And they'd always say no, we could only go after we'd traipsed round the boring stuff. Sections like Compost and Tools and Pest Control. When we finally got to Sheds, we'd be in such a state, we'd race up and down the rows (we called them streets) dashing in and out of different doors, as if we were doing a house-to-house search. And we'd choose our favourites. Some had real little staircases, leading to real upper floors; some had verandas; some, window boxes planted with plastic flowers.

Oh, I used to love Lampwick's. Not any more, though: I'd outgrown it. And outgrown it, apparently, without Mum and Dad noticing.

Because today, as soon as we'd parked, Mum said, 'Right, then!' and led us to Sheds straight away, which was unheard of. I think she expected us all to be keen. Only one of us actually was.

Timmy began trying doors at once. I stuck my hands in my pockets and shuffled along behind Mum and Dad. I didn't dare look at Bogsy. I could hear Dad asking him what his favourite subjects were at school.

We wound up in front of a largish structure called 'Shed 'n' Playhouse Under One Roof'. Dad called Timmy to come, and he emerged from Little Red Riding Hood's cottage, and joined us.

'What d'you think of this one?' said Dad.

'Quite nice,' said Timmy. 'But Little Red Riding Hood's is better. It's got curtains inside.'

'You haven't even looked inside this one,' said Dad. 'Go on. Go in and see.'

The Shed 'n' Playhouse Under One Roof was divided into two. Half was clearly a normal shed with a normal window and door; half had a child-sized door and a heart-shaped window with bright red shutters. Timmy went into this half. Even he could only just get through the door without stooping. He closed it behind him.

We waited in silence a while, then, 'Go and see what he's up to, Alex,' said Mum.

I stepped forward and peered through the window. Timmy was sitting on a small wooden chair, at a small wooden table, talking to a brown teddy bear sitting opposite him.

'He's playing bears,' I said. 'There's a bear in there.'

'Good. Very good,' said Dad, rubbing his hands. 'Timmy! Come out now! We've got something to say! Something to bring a smile to the faces of all you shed connoisseurs!'

Timmy came out with the bear in his arms.

'Guess what!' said Dad, all excited. 'No, you'd never guess!' He raised his eyebrows. '*Mum and I have decided to buy this!* Have it delivered and set up in the garden. How about that? We'll keep gardening stuff in the shed half and the other half will be yours, to do with as you like. What do you think?'

I heard a choking sound behind me. Bogsy was trying not to laugh.

Mum said that if we felt heart-shaped shutters were over the top, they could be removed.

Timmy started to say that he still thought Little Red

Riding Hood's cottage was best, but Mum cut him off: 'The bear comes with it,' she said quickly. 'The bear will be yours.'

'Really?' gasped Timmy. 'Does she, *really*?' He said no more.

'Excuse me,' I said. 'Have I got this right? You two have the grown-ups' bit, Timmy has the playhouse and I get Don's shed to myself?'

'Not quite. You and Timmy *share* your half . . .' said Mum.

'If you can fit in!' said Bogsy.

She flashed him a look. 'You'll find it's quite spacious inside. Anyway, now you two big boys have interests elsewhere, and David's shed . . .'

'So who gets Don's?'

'The new shed is going where Don's shed is now.'

'But you can't move Don's shed!' I exclaimed. Why were they being so stupid? 'It's made of bricks. It would fall apart.'

'Alex, it's falling apart already,' said Mum. 'Haven't you noticed? There's some sort of infestation in the walls

– a creature that gnaws the mortar. Maisie's son told us about it. It isn't active during the winter, but it'll be back.'

The nibbler, yes. Donald's mason bee. He had started to tell me about it, too, that first time I met him. Suddenly I remembered his voice being drowned out by Maisie's strange coughing. He'd been starting to tell me about Mum's big idea.

I knew what the idea was now. Why Maisie had stopped Donald going any further. Mum had stopped herself on the very same subject when I interrupted her talking to Dad in the kitchen that time.

'Let's get rid of the creature, then!' I could hear my voice rising. It seemed like years ago that I'd thought of the nibbler as my friend.

'I'm afraid it's too late for that now,' said Mum. 'The brickwork's in a terrible state.'

'Well, repair it!' I shouted, not caring that Bogsy would see me getting upset. 'That's easy. Get someone to come and fill in the holes.'

'Alex, Alex, calm down. If that were practical, yes, we would. But your dad and I believe the simplest solution is to start again from scratch.' She glanced towards the stupid Shed 'n' Playhouse.

I tried very hard to calm down. 'Mum, don't buy it yet. Please. I'll fix Don's shed, if you give me a chance. I'll do it! I will!'

'How will you?' Mum said gently. 'Be realistic, Alex. You wouldn't know where to begin.'

True. I wouldn't. But *somebody* would. Right now he was staring uncomfortably off towards the restaurant area, embarrassed by the scene unfolding around him.

If only his dad hadn't left, there'd be no problem; Don's shed would have been a nice job for them both. Now I'd have to try to persuade him to help me on his own. I probably could, though. When we'd finished the wings, we'd be looking around for the next thing to do.

'They used to do toasties here,' said Bogsy to nobody in particular. 'Do they still? I fancy a toastie.'

They did do toasties. All of us had one, not just him. Mum and Dad didn't buy the Shed 'n' Playhouse, either. They might have been planning to, after lunch, only Timmy felt ill, so we went straight home. He felt ill because they'd let him have this massive slice of chocolate cake. They'd offered a slice to me – and Bogsy – or a doughnut or *anything we wanted*. But I wouldn't be bought off: I had an apple. (Bogsy had an apple, too, but only because he liked them.) I knew if I didn't waver, then Mum and Dad would give me a chance. Although so often they didn't get the point, they weren't unfair. When we'd finished work on the wings, I'd speak to Bogsy.

CHAPTER 21

HALLOWEEN

Bogsy was not only proud, he was also a very secretive person. Over that week, we had a great time, but still there were things I was not allowed to know. I knew that the Icarus Show was coming. November 2nd was next Monday: that soon. I knew that Bogsy was going to fly, though I didn't know where.

Maisie was still against it, but seemed more relaxed than she'd been before. It would all be all right in the end, she said, now Bogsy and me were friends.

But were we? He still wouldn't tell me the plan.

Also, there was a secret in the freezer.

The wings were in the freezer, of course, one on top of the other, but they were *our* secret. We shared them. I mean there was something else, a secret Bogsy was keeping from me. I knew this because every time we brought out wing number two to work on, I noticed it seemed higher up than before. We no longer had to reach in so far to get it.

'What's down there?' I said to Bogsy. 'What's under *that* one –' I pointed to wing number one – 'right at the bottom?'

'Not much,' he said.

Having let me in on such a lot, perhaps he'd had to come up with something else he could keep hidden. Old habits die hard.

Although I spent most of my time next door, I realized, as the week went on, that Timmy was getting excited. He kept going out to the shops with his friends and coming back with plastic axes and severed fingers and tubes of fake blood. Mum looked alarmed at the blood and said did he realize it wouldn't wash out? He was only – *only* – to use it in the kitchen. She herself had bought a big bag of chocolate spiders, which she put at the ready, beside the front door.

Halloween was on Saturday. In the morning, Timmy carved a pumpkin (badly) and put it outside to show we were happy to join in the fun. There was no pumpkin outside the Marshes', though Bogsy, I thought, would have carved a good one.

I didn't go round to The Laurels; I went round his, to work on wing number two, instead. And when I got there, even he seemed excited. I thought it was because we were so near the end.

'Will we finish today?' I said.

'Easy!' He actually clapped his hands, just once, which he'd never done before.

'You should stick some green feathers on this one, then. You know, to match the ones on the other. You haven't put any on this one, so far.'

'None left,' said Bogsy.

'Yes, there are,' I said. I picked up the Native American headdress, which had been tossed into a corner. A lot of the feathers had gone by now – and, yes, all the green ones. He was right.

'That's funny,' I said. 'I could have sworn . . .'

But Bogsy wasn't listening.

'When I've finished, I'll do the harness,' he said, and clapped his hands again.

The very last feather was grey, like the first one I'd found in my bag, going home on the bus, that long-ago day.

'Dummy,' said Bogsy later. 'You!' and just for a moment, I felt insulted. Then I realized he meant a tailor's dummy, or one of those life-sized figures you see in shop windows, modelling clothes. He got me to put on an old rucksack frame and do up the buckle over my chest. Then he offered up the newly finished wing and I had to hold it against my arm. It felt light and scratchy.

And then he was fiddling about with bits of string and a pair of scissors. He even had a needle and thread, which he seemed quite good with. He sewed on a wristband and two wider straps, above and below my elbow. He stood at my shoulder and prodded and stitched and pulled. He was sewing me in, as I stood there; stitching me up. And when he drew back, the wing was attached to my arm in three separate places and – up by my shoulder – to the rucksack frame. It hurt me, where the straps bit in, but I didn't mind. It was like a dream. I didn't dare speak. All I could do to express my feelings was wiggle my fingers.

He noticed at once.

'Handholds!' he said and got to work again with his needle and thread. He sewed on an old dog collar for me to grip.

And then he repeated it all with the other wing, fixing it on to the opposite side. It was lucky they were so light because the whole operation took ages. Each time a thread broke or a knot came undone, he grunted, went back and redid that bit. But at last he stepped away and said, 'There!'

I was Bird Boy. At least, I was proof that Bird Boy's time had nearly come.

He told me to bend my arms, and I found that the wings were jointed in just the right places. (They pinched a bit, but nothing too bad.) He told me to flap them – slowly – to test the strength of his stitching. 'Don't worry, you won't fly away!' he said. 'Just mind you don't break them.'

And so, nervously at first, I started to move my arms

up and down. There was hardly room in the shed to stretch them out. When I did, the tip of the wing on the right brushed the painted suns on the wall. But the stitching was strong and, although the wristbands slipped slightly, I tightened my grip on the handholds, so that was OK. I could feel real air resistance and wondered if birds feel something similar (only a thousand times more) when they fly.

Bogsy was triumphant. *'Perfect!'* he said.

But I wouldn't have said so.

Don't worry, you won't fly away seemed an odd reassurance. Don't worry, you *will* fly away, more like! But Bogsy was right, though the wings were great, they'd need to be a thousand – no, a *million* – times more powerful before they'd lift someone off the ground. I was a boy, not a bird, and although I was skinny, I'd never been so aware of my *weight*.

Had he overlooked something? No, he was far too clever. He had a plan. And if he wasn't revealing it, well, never mind. I already knew the most important thing: that it would work.

'Throw yourself forward,' said Bogsy, 'as hard as you can.'

With one hand, he'd grasped the strap that went over my back; with the other, he had a hold of the doorframe. He braced himself.

'Try to break free! Go on, use all your strength!'

I lunged, but was held in check by the harness – that and Bogsy's restraining hand. Nothing snapped, nothing gave.

'Good to go!' he said.

Those were the tests he ran. That was how he satisfied himself that the wings were ready.

When I got home it was dark and Timmy had lit our pumpkin and gone. He'd left the contents of the dressing-up box all over the kitchen floor. He'd gone with his trick-or-treat friends – and Dad. Dad's job would be to hover, so people knew someone responsible was in charge. That's what dads did. That way, no one got scared (neither the people who opened their doors, nor the trick-or-treaters themselves). I could hardly remember a time in my life when Halloween had been scary.

So when someone rang our bell, it wasn't exciting, just the first in what I guessed would be a long series of tedious interruptions.

'Get that, will you?' called Mum. She was trying to tidy up the kitchen. 'Don't let them go before I get there!'

I opened the door, resolving to be unavailable next time she asked.

'Trick or Treat!' chorused two small ghosts, a witch and a little tiny zombie.

Mum bustled up. She loved this kind of thing.

'Ooh, how frightening!' she said. She hugged herself and shivered.

In the background, I saw Mr Tanner from over the road.

'Don't worry, it's only me, Mrs Meadows!' came little John Tanner's voice then, and up went the zombie mask and there he was.

'Well, thank goodness for *that*!' beamed Mum and handed round spiders.

The next time the bell went, I was watching TV and said, 'Sorry, I can't, I'm busy!' when she asked me to get it. By the third time, she didn't even ask, but hurried straight into the hall to get it herself.

She was having a ball. At each visit, she gasped in fear, then amazement and, ultimately, relief. I only hoped she'd bought enough chocolate to last the night.

Because callers kept on coming. Here was *another* ring on the bell. I started unwrapping a spider I'd found dropped down the side of the sofa. It was only the foil that made it a spider; inside it was just a smooth chocolate ball that could have been anything. At Christmas they probably wrapped them in red, to look like Rudolf's nose. *Typical*, I thought, and popped the chocolate into my mouth.

And that's when Mum screamed. It wasn't a long or a loud scream, but I could tell it wasn't put on. It was real.

'Alex, come here a sec, would you,' she called, trying to sound as if it was nothing, but not succeeding.

There was only one caller, not a group. And no reassuring dad in the background. It wasn't a little kid, either: the figure at the door was as tall as me.

I knew who it was straight away. He was wearing the wings.

But the wings hung down at his sides and weren't what you noticed.

It was the mask.

No wonder Mum was frightened.

The head of a bird, with a huge, hooked beak and bulging, vengeful eyes. In secret, he'd made something monstrous. A bunch of green feathers stuck up from the top.

'Who is it?' said Mum, though whether to him or to me wasn't clear.

'It's all right,' I said. 'I know who it is.'

And the bird said, 'You coming?' His voice was muffled but echoey, too.

'I don't think Alex . . .' Mum said weakly. 'Here, let me give you a chocolate spider.'

While she was fiddling with the bag, I nipped back down the hall to the kitchen. She hadn't got far with the tidying job. I grabbed up a Frankenstein mask from the floor, then nipped back. 'I'll be fine!' I said, slipping past her to join the figure on the step.

Poor Mum – she'd had such a good evening, till now. 'Don't be long!' she told me, but she must have known I'd be just as long as I liked.

'Don't worry!' I said.

As we went down the path, 'Get your bike!' said Bogsy in his new, bird voice.

'We don't need bikes.'

'We might,' he said, and I saw he'd got his, propped up by the gate.

So I went round the side of the house to fetch mine and, when I came back, he was already ringing the bell at the Tanners' front door. It was too late for me to go with him.

I saw the door open; I heard Mrs Tanner scream, just like Mum. Then I heard the door slam.

He came back and got his bike. 'She shut the door.'

'Of course she did!' I said. 'She was frightened. You should have waited for me!'

We wheeled our bikes up the road till we came to the next lit Jack-o'-lantern. Old Mrs Chittenden's house. She'd had her grandchildren for half-term.

We knocked her knocker. *Rat-a-tat-tat*.

Old Mrs Chittenden opened the door and stared at Bogsy. 'Oh – *dear*!' She put a hand to her throat and started backing into the room.

Quickly I whipped off my Frankenstein mask. 'Don't worry, it's me, Alex Meadows, from down the road!'

'Alex? Is it really? Well, that's a relief! For a moment, I thought . . .' She glanced at Bogsy, tall and silent, standing beside me.

She gave me a couple of fairy cakes, iced in green, with bat-shaped sprinkles on top.

After Mrs Chittenden, 'Let's visit *her* now,' said Bogsy.

'Who?'

'You know. *Her*.'

He never referred to Maisie by name.

'We can't go round to The Laurels,' I said. 'They'd all die of heart attacks! If that's what we brought our bikes for, you can forget it.'

'It's not,' he said. But he seemed to accept that we weren't going round Maisie's.

We wheeled the bikes on. We called at several more houses and the same thing happened at each: people were scared until I removed my mask. Then, whether or not they knew me, they calmed down enough to give us treats. It was good I was there. Sometimes we met other groups of trick-or-treaters on the pavement. The little kids pointed at Bogsy and the dads moved protectively close.

We were three or four streets away from our own when I started wondering how many more? It was cold.

'One more,' said Bogsy.

He led the way into the Sancton estate and stopped outside a largish house behind a high, dense hedge. He let his bike fall against the hedge and adjusted his wings. But there was no Jack-o'-lantern.

'We can't do this one,' I objected.

'Who says?'

'There's no pumpkin.'

'No one to tell us to go away, then.'

There was a gate in the hedge, a tall one, all curly iron bars, and Bogsy was doing something – *clink clink clink* – to the catch.

'Won't it open?' I asked him, hoping it wouldn't.

'It'll open for now,' he said. 'Come on, let's go,' and we walked up the path.

He rang the bell and we waited on the step. There was definitely no pumpkin.

A man I'd never seen before came to the door and stared at us, frowning.

I went to take off my mask, but Bogsy stopped me.

'Hey!' the man called, back into the house. 'Hey! Get off the computer! This one's for you!'

No answer.

'You coming, or what? Take those headphones off!'

And someone came. Someone in socks and a Simpsons T-shirt, padding along the passage to stand by his dad. It was Alan Tydman.

I wasn't prepared. Neither was Alan. Neither, perhaps, was Bogsy himself. It was one of those situations where you have to see what happens and then react. For someone who'd trained himself *not* to react, it was hard. But then, it was hard for us all.

And for two or three seconds, nothing happened.

196

Then, suddenly, Alan yelled, 'BIRD BOY!' really loud, like he was firing a starter's pistol – and, like somebody running a race, Bogsy was off.

Everything happened very fast after that. Alan bent down and I saw he was trying to get on a pair of shoes. Which was a mistake. It gave me my chance. I turned and ran back down the path. Bogsy was waiting outside the gate and when I got through it he clanged it shut and bent down and there was a *clink* and a *click*, and I realized he'd snapped shut a padlock.

'Bikes!' he gasped. We almost fell over each other to get them and mount them and *go*!

Before we reached the end of the road, we heard pounding footsteps behind us on the pavement. Alan must either have climbed the gate or pushed through the hedge. And when we turned out of his road, into the next, the footsteps came on.

He was gaining on us. He actually was.

I knew he was a fast runner (he was unbeatable in athletics) but hadn't realized *how* fast – till that night. I wondered if Bogsy had factored it in. We were doing

197

right-hand turns without slowing or signalling, desperately cutting corners by going on the pavement whenever we could. One time I took the curb badly and nearly came off. Would Alan have stopped and torn off my mask? I had the feeling he wouldn't have bothered, obsessed, as he was, with one thing.

'BIRD BOY!' he shouted again. 'I'LL GET YOU!'

But he didn't, not that night. He kept up his speed for several streets (when we came to our own, Lark Lane, we had to go past it) but then he slowed down. And soon after that, we lost him. We wound our way back by a different route.

Timmy's Jack-o'-lantern had gone out. Not that I went home. I followed Bogsy and flung down my bike beside his, in his front garden. Bogsy took off his mask and poked his normal, Bogsy head in through the door to see if his mum was around.

She was upstairs, so we hurried straight through.

In the shed, he took off his wings. They must have been hard to cycle in. They'd have caught the wind: he'd done well to go as fast as he had. I wasn't surprised he was panting. I pulled off the Frankenstein mask, which my breath had made wet and slimy inside.

It was dark in the shed, of course, but there was a moon and its light slanted in through the window. We could see that the wings were undamaged by our flight. Even the tuft of green feathers on top of his mask was still there.

We lay on our backs in the mess on the floor with our arms outstretched – like kids in the snow, making angels – and laughed and laughed.

As if everything was OK.

Just because we'd survived.

CHAPTER 22
LAST DAY

The next day was both the last day of half-term and the first of November. When I went round Bogsy's shed, he showed me a pile of paper slips. At last I was going to find out where the show would take place.

But no, I wasn't. When I put out a hand to turn a slip over, Bogsy shot his out and knocked mine away. It was like when I'd tried to stick on a feather, the first time we'd worked on the wing.

'You'll get one as usual,' he said. 'Except you'll get two.'

'Why two?' The strangeness of that did away with the disappointment.

'One for you, one for her.'

'Oh!'

I wasn't sure Maisie would want a note. She'd rejected a feather when he'd offered her one. She wanted nothing to do with the Icarus Show. But I'd give it a try.

'When will you hand them out?' I asked.

'Tomorrow. End of the day. Take hers then.'

Not, Would you be free after school tomorrow, to deliver Maisie's note? He'd never say that. But I didn't mind. I was used to his way of talking.

And suddenly now I thought I could ask him about rebuilding Don's shed.

'After the show . . .' I began, but he gave me such an odd look that I faltered. 'After the show . . . I was wondering . . . if you could help . . .'

He began saying no, without letting me finish. But the very unfairness of that gave me an idea.

'Seeing as I've helped *you*!' I said loudly.

Even Bogsy must see *that* was fair. And he did.

'I would,' he said, 'but I won't be . . .' *He* was the one to hesitate now! '. . . I won't be around.'

Where would he be? Oh, wait – of course! He'd have flown away! I smiled.

'Ha ha!' I said.

Our last afternoon together in the shed we spent – guess what – tidying! Bogsy, the world's messiest person, said he wanted a clear-out! He dragged a wheelie bin round to the door and scooped up an armful of rubbish and chucked it in.

'Hey!' I protested. 'You just threw away an unopened packet of gum! I saw!'

'Good!' he said.

After that, I didn't try to help. He didn't need help with throwing stuff out. What he needed was someone there watching, to make sure nothing important got trashed.

Because Bogsy went into a kind of frenzy. At first I thought he was just being careless, not checking to see what was going in the bin. But after a while, I came to think he was glorying in the abandon. He picked up his wonderful Halloween mask and held it above his head.

'Not that!' I cried. 'Don't bin that! You could wear it tomorrow!'

'No point. It wasn't for real.'

'But it goes with the wings!'

'It goes *here*!' and he smashed it down in the rubbish, green feathers first. 'Gone! History!' He seemed elated.

Next time I was quicker. He grabbed up some things, one of which, I saw, was a book. I darted forward and swiped it.

It was his English exercise book. He'd written his own and Mr Smith's name on the cover. I was shocked – and not just because he'd been throwing it away.

'Homework!' I gasped. 'Have you done it?' I hadn't. All that week, no thought of school had entered my head. But now I was worried.

'We had to write a poem, remember? We've got English tomorrow afternoon!'

'Tomorrow?' He laughed disdainfully. 'Bin it!'

But the thought of homework not yet done had spoiled things for me. Mr Smith gave out detentions to people who didn't hand homework in.

'Let's stop and do our poems,' I said. 'It won't take long, they don't have to be good.'

But he wouldn't. What's more, he snatched back his book and this time binned it for real.

He could always retrieve it and write his poem when I'd gone, when he'd come to his senses. I hoped he would, but I never found out if he did or not.

CHAPTER 23
IRONY

Too late I remembered that it was Bogsy's birthday. The fact it was Icarus Day had eclipsed the birthday, in my mind. I'd meant to get him some *peppermint* gum, for a joke – it would have been good – but I couldn't now. It was halfway through Monday morning and even if Year 7s *had* been allowed down the shops, I'd got no money.

Well, I'd got my money for lunch, but what was the use of that when we weren't allowed out? (It was true, there were Year 11s who'd buy you things if you paid up front; but often they kept the change, and sometimes even the things themselves.)

And then I had a clever idea. I could use a bit of my lunch money to buy sweets off Alan.

Buying sweets off Alan on Icarus Day, you might think would be risky. What's more, my plan had been to not buy anything off him ever again. My plan had been to hang out with Bogsy and not mind who saw. But we hadn't sat together on the bus because there were only single seats left, and we hadn't sat together in form time or maths because then our places were fixed. Break would have been our first chance to hang out.

But at break time I went off with Alan and Rob: for the very last time, it would be. Bogsy would understand as soon as I gave him his birthday present. I don't even know if he saw me go off.

My main concern, in approaching Alan today, was to keep my head on. Others obviously felt the same way, and were not approaching at all. Which meant that at least he'd have plenty of sweets to sell.

I considered handing over *all* my money, but decided not to. The amount you paid had little or nothing to do with what you got back: that depended on other, unknowable things. And today was Icarus Day, after all. *Anything* could happen. When I gave him my money,

I kept enough back to buy pizza at lunch.

And so I was doubly amazed when he brought out a bag so full that it wouldn't even close!

While Rob and Jack stood by – and poor Andy P looked longingly on – he held it out with his two hands cupped, to prevent things spilling from the top. I could see cola chews and one end of a flump and a blue-and-green jelly snake. And as he put it in my two hands, another amazing thing happened. He winked! He looked right into my eyes and winked one of his: there could be no mistake. I wasn't sure I could wink back, so I just said, 'Thanks! *Thanks*, Al.'

And he said, 'No worries – Al!' and laughed. 'Hey! *Al!* You and me both!'

It was overwhelming. One minute I was Bed-ows, the weirdo who couldn't get up in the morning. The next, I was in there with Alan Tydman – right in, right up there, like Rob Bone and Jack.

I never found out why he did that, that day. Perhaps the tension had made him go funny. Or maybe he'd guessed it was me in the Frankenstein mask on Halloween night and thought I might lead him to Icarus if he invited me in.

Whatever it was, it had the effect of dragging me back. Like a swimmer at sea being dragged off course by the tide. The tide – Alan Tydman. Ha! Mr Smith would perhaps have a word for that.

I had two: bad luck. Alan had tipped me the wink just when I thought I'd put him behind me, made up my mind that Bogsy was best.

Bogsy *was* best, but the little white bag overflowing with sweets was exciting, too. True, it would make a good birthday present, but that wasn't all. I had to admit, I wanted to taste – just *taste* – what properly being in Alan's Battalion was like.

At lunchtime, Alan and Rob and the rest took their food to the science wall. I took my slice of pizza. Tomorrow I'd find out where Bogsy spent lunch, and go there (even if it was Chess Club). After today, I'd never set foot in Tydman territory again.

But when we came round the corner of Science, it was occupied already. There, where he shouldn't have been

– where he never had been before – *was* Bogsy. He was leaning against the wall.

He was whistling and looking about him in a casual kind of way, like he was waiting for a bus. When we drew nearer, he just kept on, as if we weren't there.

I was glad about that. He might not notice me.

And Alan and Rob exchanged a glance. This is it, I thought, Alan's fuse: it's been lit. It was always going to be, someday or other – and this was Icarus Day. *I* could have lit it, Jack could've, Peter Horn could've, or Andy P. The fact it was Bogsy meant nothing. The only odd thing was the way he had *made* it be him.

The rest of us – me, Jack and two or three others (me trying to keep myself hidden behind them) – came to a stop, but Alan and Rob threw their chips on the ground and moved forward. The two of them went to stand next to him, one on each side, very close, pressing shoulder to shoulder. Standing shoulder to shoulder with someone usually means you're on their side. But Alan and Rob were a hostile force, crushing Bogsy between them. It must have hurt. They were leaning against the wall, but also leaning inwards, hard. Bogsy looked small. But he carried on whistling.

'Bit noisy here today,' said Alan.

'Bit smelly,' said Rob.

'Bit *crowded*,' said Alan.

Bogsy hadn't moved while they spoke – and then, all of a sudden, he did. He bent his knees to release his shoulders and stepped away from the wall. It happened so quickly that Alan and Rob fell in on each other, clunking heads. It could have been funny, but wasn't, and nobody laughed. Bogsy started strolling away.

'OI!' bellowed Alan. 'Disturb you, did we?'

Bogsy didn't reply.

'What's your problem?' Alan tried again.

'My problem?' said Bogsy, over his shoulder. 'My problem is finding a place to go where there aren't Neanderthals!'

'*I'll tell you where you can go,*' said Alan, '*if you come back here.*' He nodded to Rob. Rob went after Bogsy and grabbed his collar and pulled him back. He marched him to Alan and made him stand still by twisting the collar, tight. Bogsy tried to get him off by thrusting back with his elbows, but Rob held on.

'What you said just now,' said Alan. 'Say it again!'

Bogsy didn't break. 'Neanderthals,' he said, hoarsely but clearly, 'in this school – are – my – problem.'

And Alan hit him. Punched him low, in the stomach. Bogsy cried out with the shock and the pain. Alan punched him again, then clutched his shirt to stop him falling. Then Bogsy was trying to hit back, but he wasn't a fighter, as I knew: the movements he made with his arms were more like the panicky movements of someone fighting their way through a field of tall grass with a snake in it – somewhere.

Rob stood back to give Alan space. Which made me think of someone delivering an animal for slaughter.

And Alan worked efficiently. He was doing what he did best. Bogsy had been wrong to write him off as a moron, I thought, because in this he was highly skilled.

It was horrible; Bogsy was squealing like a pig.

But as I watched, I realized this: that Alan was beating

up Icarus. He was doing what he'd always wanted, and he didn't even know! Mr Smith would have called that irony. He'd have loved it. (Well, not the fight.) And the most ironic thing was that when it was finished and Bogsy was hammered, even then, Icarus would have won.

I didn't think to run for a teacher till Alan hit Bogsy right in the face and suddenly there was blood. It's against the rules to go for the face; if somebody does, they've gone too far. Bogsy dropped down with his arms round his head to try to protect it and, just as I left, I saw Jack nip in and kick him – hard – as he lay there, curled up, on the ground.

Oddly enough, the first teacher I spotted in the playground *was* Mr Smith, and before I was even halfway through my story, he'd started running. He ran to Science so fast that he left me behind. I heard his furious shout, round the corner, before I'd got there myself, and by the time I had, thanks to him, everything was over.

Bogsy could stand, he could even walk, though he looked a mess.

'Who'll go with David to the medical room?' said Mr Smith, but no one volunteered.

I wanted to, I really did. I could hear Maisie's voice in my head: *someone who'll stand by you.* And what made it worse was that Bogsy was staring at me.

Ever since he'd got back up on his feet, he'd been doing it. Even before, from the moment he'd first thought it safe to uncover his head. Staring and staring. Nobody seemed to notice, with Mr Smith shouting, and Alan still high as a kite.

And when, in the end, Mr Smith led him off to the medical room himself, Bogsy twisted his head round to look back over his shoulder, one last time. I couldn't interpret the look. But it made me feel really, really bad.

And he wasn't in school in the afternoon. He must have gone home.

CHAPTER 24

ISAAC NEWTON

I was on the school bus, going home that day, when I found it. I opened my bag to get out my book, and spotted it straight away. It was tucked inside the secret pocket where I keep my spare pen and my money for lunch. Of course there was no change today, but the pocket was bulging, as that's where I'd put the bag of sweets. He must have seen the sweets: he'd tucked his envelope behind them.

I wasn't worried about that. I'd take them round to him later on. I was far more worried about the look he'd given me in the playground. What I was doing there with Alan, why I'd hung back when I could have stepped forward: those things would be more difficult to explain.

But once I had, everything would be fine.

I didn't open the envelope at once. His final note. I'd open it just as I'd opened his first: in private. I stood in our garden, thinking, First and last, beginning and end. A late apple fell just in front of me, and hit the brick path with a juicy smack. It had started to rot on the tree, and lay, split open, in the mess of its own brown pulp. I stepped over it on my way to Don's shed.

I sat on my old wooden box. In a way, it *was* like that very first time. But now there was no sensation of being watched. (Not even the spider seemed to be there.) And now I knew what I would find: the place. The last bit of information.

As I unsealed the flap, I tried to think of good places to fly a kite. They had to be wide and open, with plenty of room to get a good run.

I took out two slips of paper (one for me, one for Maisie) but didn't yet let myself look at the words.

The run was important to give that upward launch. I pictured a field, maybe even the playing field at school. A hill would be good, but there weren't any hills round here.

And then I looked.

I looked at both slips, just in case they were different; they were the same. Although the words were in English, they didn't make sense.

I thought of the apple falling from the tree and smashing on the path. I looked at the words on the bits of paper again, and now I could read them.

'Motorway bridge. Southbound carriageway side.'

I began to understand.

Everyone knew the motorway bridge: an ugly straight line, crossing high over Hinton Road. You'd be mad to take a kite there. It would be way too dangerous for that. It wasn't a place for an upward launch, but a downward drop. I thought of Mr Smith's sticky brown mixture of beeswax and blood, just before half-term. He'd been talking about Icarus, of course. Icarus's end.

I banged out of Don's shed and sprinted back up the path, leaping the split-open apple. We'd done Isaac Newton at school, so I knew that falling apples could teach you a lot. Isaac had seen one and understood gravity:

so had I. I'd seen what would happen if you jumped off a motorway bridge with a hard, tarmac surface below. Wings or no wings.

And I had to get to Bogsy. I had to make sure his plan took that into account. I know how stupid it sounds, but you see I was hoping I was wrong about the bridge.

Each time I'd done something over the past few weeks, I'd thought I was doing something big. But I wasn't. The Do Nothing kid I'd heard Mum talk about: I knew who he was.

And I thought I'd changed. But I hadn't. Till now.

I rushed straight round to Bogsy's front door and rang the bell.

And only then, as I waited, did I consider how his mum might be feeling about the fight.

What if she was angry? What if she'd had to take Bogsy to hospital? I hoped she had. If they kept him in hospital overnight, at least he'd be safe. And if she stayed there with him, I wouldn't have to face her now.

She hadn't taken him to hospital. But, when she opened the door, she didn't seem angry. Far from it.

'Oh, Alex!' she said. 'You *are* a good friend. Thanks for coming. I knew you would!'

'I need to see him,' I said. 'Right now.'

'Yes, of course. He's down in the shed.' She hurried me through.

There were several unopened birthday presents and cards on the living room table. I half wished I'd brought the bag of sweets, but perhaps it was best I'd not.

'You mustn't worry,' she said. 'He really isn't as bad as he looks. I'll bring down some biscuits – no, *cake* – in a while.'

He *looked* totally awful. They'd tried to clean him up, but the blood from his face had got into his hair – and they hadn't washed that. (Perhaps he hadn't let them.) It had dried dull black and made the hair clump together in an awkward way on one side.

And his face! Half of it was so swollen that the eye was shut. Bruises are meant to be black and blue, but Bogsy's face was green. He looked like a ghoul. He could have gone trick-or-treating without a mask and still scared everyone.

Now I was in the shed with him, I couldn't think how to begin. Not by saying Happy Birthday, that was for sure. He fixed me with his one good eye, but didn't try to help.

'Your mum seemed pleased to see me,' I ventured.

'She thinks you're my friend.'

'Well . . .' I didn't want to get into this. The atmosphere was tense.

'I've told her,' said Bogsy. 'Only cretins and thugs at that school.'

'But what about me?'

'*Only cretins and thugs.*'

'But I'm not like the others!'

'No?' He jutted his swollen face forward and pointed.

'That wasn't me!'

'You were there!'

'Only because . . . I was going to . . .'

It sounded feeble. I knew he wouldn't believe me.

And yet I hoped one day he would.

'And this?' He lifted his shirt. Another great bruise spread over his ribs.

'*That* wasn't me!'

'Well, it wasn't Rob Bonebrain.'

'It was Jack!'

'Yeah?' said Bogsy.

He thought it was me! Now I knew what that look in the playground had meant.

'It was me who went and got Mr Smith! You can ask him! As I was going, I saw Jack . . .'

Bogsy looked at me shrewdly, as he'd looked at me once before, in this shed. But before, he had looked with two eyes, instead of just one. I waited in silence. Before, there'd been slips of paper to signal the end of his calculations.

There were no slips of paper this time – not counting the ones scrunched up in my pocket – nothing to show what he'd decided. When he finished staring and bit into an apple, I hadn't a clue.

But I'd nothing to lose.

'I came to say something important.'

'Don't bother,' he said. He took a step forward, so I took one back.

'Your note . . .'

Another step forward, and another back towards the door, for me.

'If you jump off that bridge tonight . . .'

One more step – and now I was outside the shed, and he'd closed the door to a crack, through which he was looking with his one good eye (which was all he needed in this situation).

'If you jump off that bridge,' I said to the eye, 'if you – jump –' the eye narrowed – 'well, it's *dangerous*.'

To my surprise, he started laughing, but it wasn't a cheerful sound.

'I just hope you've got a good plan!' I said desperately.

But he'd shut the door.

CHAPTER 25

MAISIE AND DONALD

As I ran to the wall of wheelie bins, I heard someone calling my name. It was Bogsy's mum. She sounded upset.

'Alex! Alex! Don't go! Please!'

She was coming carefully down the garden, holding something against her chest, protecting it with her arm. I realized it was his cake and she was trying to keep the candles alight.

I pulled the bins apart and dived through. I landed on an actual pumpkin, a big one, and felt it split, but ran on, up our garden.

I would have told Mr Smith *now*, if I could. He'd have sorted this out. But he would have gone home from school by now, and I'd no idea where he lived. There was only once place to go, one person to help me.

Maisie had been right all along. She was always right. She'd seen danger. I'd barely seen past the end of my nose!

The bus might not come for half an hour, so I got out my bike and started to cycle.

Maisie would say, I Told You So. If only she'd been more insistent! She'd seen how things were. It was all her fault!

But, of course, it wasn't. I'd thought I knew best. Donald had urged me on, too. When I got to The Laurels today, he'd probably make some ridiculous joke about how come I hadn't brought him a slice of birthday cake?

But when I turned into the car park, I knew that Donald couldn't be there. There was nothing banana-coloured in sight. Which was good: I'd have Maisie all to myself.

Confusingly, though, when I knocked on her door, it was Donald who called, 'Come in!'

Straight away, I knew something had changed. I'd missed last Saturday's visit – that's all it took – and they'd gone and done something behind my back. Although I'd done things behind theirs, I didn't expect them to do the same. And yet they had. Something was definitely different in Maisie's room.

It reminded me of a book Auntie Jen once sent, called *The Railway Children*. According to her, it was Timeless; according to me, it was just very old. But the last page must have stuck in my head. The long lost dad came back to the family home, and went in through the door. That's it. Why it was memorable was the reader wasn't allowed to go with him: we were left outside. They'd got their happy ending in there, and everything was so lovely for them, they didn't want us around. It choked you up.

I'd never felt unwanted when I'd been to visit Maisie. The times I'd been turned away, in the old days, it had been by the person in reception, never her. And then when Donald had come, the two of them always made me welcome. But now, although Donald had said come in, I felt there was a second door, shutting me out, an invisible one. Maisie had obviously been crying, but not in the old sad way, I thought. Donald was holding her hand, though she pulled it away as soon as she saw me. I felt I'd intruded on something and wanted to leave.

But I did what I tended to do on occasions like this: said something stupid.

'Where's your car?' I asked Donald.

'In the car park.'

'It isn't,' I said.

'Ah, hawk-eye!' He smiled. 'You don't miss much! You're right, the banana's not there: I took it back to the hire place today and got a new one.'

'A new banana?'

'No! I bought something decent, from a garage.'

'Oh.'

'You know why?'

I shrugged. 'Had enough of . . .'

'*No!* The point is I *bought* one. Come on! Why d'you think I'd do that?'

'Now who's teasing!' said Maisie. 'Just tell him.'

'Well . . .'

But she didn't let him say. 'The great booby!' She

actually clapped her hands and laughed. 'He's not going back to Australia!'

'Ma's been missing me.'

'Nonsense!' said Maisie.

But he just said quietly, 'She needs me. So I'm staying.'

Now it made sense, this feeling I had. This was their happy ending. I was supposed to shut the book.

It may have been theirs; it wasn't mine, though. What if I made them listen to *me*? I could say I was sorry for not having listened to Maisie, then show them the final Icarus message. They had to help; no one else could.

And yet they were no longer interested. They obviously hadn't even remembered that this was November 2nd.

I stood in the doorway and knew it was hopeless. All I could think of was shouting, *How d'you make someone change their mind?*

Because that's what it came down to, really. Just that.

Maisie must know. She'd made Donald. What was the trick?

And as I stood there, Maisie stepped in.

'What've you been up to, then? Anything interesting to report?'

I couldn't think where to begin. There was far too much. It would take too long. But I tried. I had to.

'He shut the door in my face.'

No, begin at the beginning.

'We went trick-or-treating,' I said, 'he made a mask, he nearly got beaten up. Then he *did* – get beaten up, I mean. There was a fight . . .'

It sounded all wrong. It was just a muddle.

And then I surprised myself by saying, 'But I know what it's all about!'

I hadn't known I did till then. It was simple, though.

'His dad left. That's what. And other things, too. But nothing he couldn't have handled . . . If his dad hadn't gone.'

'Oh!' said Maisie. 'I see.'

'He gave these out today,' I said, pulling the slips of paper from my pocket. I handed one to Donald and one to her, as I didn't need mine any more.

'Get my specs, Alex, please, from the table,' she said. Then she read the note.

A short silence followed, while they both took in the words.

'Well,' said Maisie then. 'This looks bad –' she reached for her necklace – 'but as you're his friend . . .'

I lost patience. '*I'm not!* That's what I'm trying to say! I messed up!'

'What did you do?' said Donald, and Maisie shushed him.

'It doesn't matter. But he'll never trust me now!'

'Never say never!' said Donald in a stupid, sing-song voice. 'There's always tomorrow . . .'

'There isn't!' I shouted. 'Today is November 2nd! Remember? Icarus Day! *He could die!*'

'Never say –'

'Donald, shut *up*!' said Maisie. 'Let's think. So he's missing his dad, is he? Well . . .'

'We can't get in touch with his dad!' I stamped my foot. 'We don't have his number.'

'We don't,' said Maisie. 'But somebody might.' She looked at me sternly. 'You need to calm down. You're overheated. It's not helping.'

'We could go for a spin in the car?' said Donald. 'Get some fresh air. I could drive you home?'

'No. I cycled. I've got my bike.' I didn't say thanks.

'Well, I hope you've got lights,' said Donald. 'You may need them.'

'What d'you mean?' But I saw what he meant. Outside the French windows, the sky was dimming. I glanced at the clock on Maisie's wall.

'It's OK, look. Still plenty of time.'

'You've forgotten,' said Donald. 'Clocks changed last week. It gets dark an hour earlier now.'

I had forgotten. No, I hadn't, I just hadn't taken any notice. I'd thought the sun could be trusted to set at six for ever and ever.

But all things change, even clocks. You'd think I'd have learned.

'Got to go!' I said. 'Got to catch him!' I suddenly saw myself standing with arms outstretched, underneath the motorway bridge, to catch Bogsy like catching a cricket ball hurtling towards me, out of the sky. But it wasn't funny. It could happen.

'I mean, got to catch him before he leaves . . .'

Maisie was holding out both hands towards me. She wasn't holding the necklace now. She'd never been *gentle* with me before. 'Alex, come here.' But I didn't have time, and she dropped her hands in her lap.

'Good luck!' she said. 'Trust your instincts. They're good.'

Wrong! My instincts were useless! If it wasn't for them, this wouldn't be happening!

'Don't think too hard!' she called after me, down the corridor. 'Keep a clear head!'

Everyone else in The Laurels would hear, but she didn't seem to mind. Maybe some of the more confused should take her advice.

CHAPTER 26
THE BRIDGE

I'd never cycled so fast in all my life. Well, perhaps I had on Halloween night, when we'd had to escape Alan Tydman. But apart from that.

When I reached the top of Lark Lane, the sun hadn't set, but that didn't mean Bogsy hadn't yet left. He'd need to leave in good enough time to be there before everyone else, wouldn't he? I wondered if I should go straight on, as he'd almost certainly be ahead by now. I stood with my bike, breathing hard, unsure what to do. And as I was trying to decide, a bike came towards me, up the lane.

When it drew level, I pushed my own bike out in front of it, so that it had to swerve and the rider nearly fell off.

'What the . . . ?!' He faced me angrily. '*You?!*'

'Sorry,' I said. And then again, '*Sorry,*' though this was for something else.

He still only had one working eye, which he fixed me with challengingly.

'You gonna mess things up?' he said, as he'd said once before.

And so we were back to square one.

Only we weren't. This time, I'd keep a clear head.

'Gonna come with you,' I said, and without really knowing what I meant: 'Gonna help you.' Maisie had said, *Don't think too hard*, so I didn't.

Bogsy was getting impatient. There was no time to argue or do sums. He muttered something I couldn't make out, but chose to think was, *Alright then*. And when he set off, I went with him and he didn't seem to mind. Or perhaps it was more that he realized it would have been pointless saying get lost.

He didn't have the wings, which was strange, but meant that we could have been any old kids from school on our way to the show.

Far away from the boys on their bikes and the show about to begin, on the far side of Burstead, a country road leads out from the town. Houses are strung out a certain way along it, and most have their lights on, their curtains drawn. The one at the end does.

The one at the end has a big square sign sticking out from the wall, and a couple of benches stacked up beneath. It isn't a house, but a pub. Nobody sits on the benches at this time of year, but inside, it's cosy. A real log fire has been lit and the first of the evening drinkers have gathered. They call to each other in cheerful voices, and take their turn at the bar.

'Hey, Titch, what's yours?' calls one of them to a man sitting by the fire.

The man by the fire has two glasses already – someone else has just bought him a second – but he grins and calls back, 'Same again!' He's come here to drown his sorrows and they're going to take a lot of drowning.

The motorway bridge goes over the road to Hinton, and that road runs through fields, with a ditch on either side.

It's a lonely road, with no houses or lights. But when we reached it, the sun hadn't set, not quite.

Approaching the bridge itself, there's a wide grass verge on the roadside, as well as the ditch. At a certain point, this was scattered with bikes, thrown down any old how, since there weren't any trees or hedges to lean them against. And not far beyond the bikes, their owners were gathered: kids from our form. Alan Tydman was there, with Rob at his side and Jack close by.

And a little apart from the kids, all except one, was an adult: a real live policeman! The one kid standing with him was Peter Horn.

Had Peter Horn called the police? Had he got them to take him seriously? And then the policeman turned round, at the sound of our brakes. There was still enough light to make out his face, and I saw it was Peter's dad. Peter Horn's dad was *in* the police! That was lucky.

We laid down our bikes with the others, and joined the thin little crowd from behind. We stood at the back. If we'd reached out our hands, we could have touched Lydia and Candy, who were in front of us, arms linked. They turned in sync and clocked us, but that was all. They didn't make a fuss about Bogsy; they didn't react to his terrible face; they showed no surprise that he'd come, so soon after the fight.

Everyone's interest was fixed on the bridge. Only Alan Tydman was making a point of looking away. Nobody gave a stuff about us. It was funny how unimportant they thought we were.

And up on the bridge, where the motorway rumbled, up there, there was nothing to see. This was the south-bound carriageway side, but the show had not begun. It couldn't, with Bogsy and me down here. That's how unimportant we were!

I shivered and not just with cold. The excitement was catching. I almost believed he *was* going to fly. I almost forgot boys can't (any more than pigs). I almost forgot what he *was* going to do.

Then I remembered and shivered again. I had to stop him, that's why I'd come. But how was I going to?

How could I possibly, all on my own?

In the pub beyond Burstead, a phone starts to ring. Phones go off all the time, of course, but this one is in a coat pocket and the coat has been hung on a hook by the door. Nobody hears it above the talking and laughter in the bar, so no one picks up. The man by the fire is on his third pint.

A parapet ran the length of the bridge, and was topped by three lines of rails, which now stood out hard and stark against the glowing sky. If he climbed up there and spread his wings, he'd look *great*. I almost wanted him to.

It was freezing now, on Hinton Road, and a wind was getting up. It came at us through the bridge, which funnelled it, giving it extra strength. People were getting restless. Was he enjoying making them wait? I looked at his face, but it was so bruised, I couldn't tell what he was thinking. (Maybe I wouldn't have been able to anyway: I never had before.)

Somebody cracked a joke (not a good one) and someone else laughed, but the laughter trailed off.

Bogsy was making fools of them all, but he shouldn't push it too far. They could easily get fed up and go home.

In the pub someone gets up to go to the loo and brushes past the coats by the door. A ringtone is coming from one of them, this person notices. Somebody's mobile, left in a pocket. Could be anyone's. Pointless to try and identify whose.

But no, it's this pocket, here, in a coat much bigger than all the rest. It needs a peg to itself, this coat, whereas all the rest have to share. Looks like it was made for a giant.

There aren't many giants around these days. There's certainly only one in the pub.

'Titch! Hey, Titch! Phone! C'mere!'

On either side of the bridge, a steep embankment led up to the motorway itself, thickly grown with fir trees. The sun was so low, it was *under* the bridge, but the sky was so bright under there, you could hardly bear to look away. When you did, the rest of the landscape seemed drab. The fir trees were a solid, dull black. You wished the sun wouldn't go.

I was so intent on that, I almost missed it.

Bogsy was slipping away! I only just noticed in time. (No one else did at all.) He'd gone from my side.

He'd detached himself from the crowd and was moving back, the way we'd come: leaving me behind.

Oh no you don't! I said to myself and hurried after him. And when he jumped down in the ditch, I was right behind him, jumping too. He wouldn't shake me off that easily. Not on his bike at the top of Lark Lane; not now. When he dropped down on to hands and knees, so did I. Because there, in the ditch, with its mouth towards us, was something that looked like a massive toilet roll tube!

A drainage pipe, it was really, stretching away towards the bridge. And it was big enough for a person.

Two.

If they went down on hands and knees.

Him and his tubes.

'What?' says the man in the pub, pressing his phone to his ear and beginning to shout. 'What did you say? I can't hear!'

Now he is standing, he towers over everyone else,

even those who are standing as well. He's huge. He knocks his head on the doorframe as he steps outside.

'Now – say again!' Although he's drunk nearly three pints, his eyes are focused, his mind alert. If he sways a bit, it's only because of that clonk as he came through the door.

He rubs his head. 'Where?'

He can hear much better out here, but he still asks for things to be repeated because he can hardly take them in.

'No! Stay where you are! I'll go!' he says fiercely. 'It has to be me.'

Then he just says, 'Jesus Christ!'

He says that a couple more times before the conversation ends.

One of his mates comes out to see if everything's OK. It may or may not be. On the small patch of tarmac under the sign (which announces the pub as The Bricklayer's Arms) there is nobody there.

It was totally black in the pipe. No encouraging light at the end of the tunnel this time. No Wonderland. I opened and closed my eyes, to see if that changed anything. It didn't. The pipe was concrete and cold (though not damp) and gritty. I hoped there weren't rats. But my main thought was not to let Bogsy give me the slip. He was moving forward, I knew from the sounds, and I knew he wasn't going to wait if I fell behind. It was scary, not being able to pause or be cautious in that dark. But at least there wasn't any danger of going the wrong way or missing a turning. There was only one way and no turning to take.

And so we crawled on. The grit and the concrete were hurting my knees. But Bogsy didn't stop. And after a while my eyes began working. I could dimly see his shape, like a bung blocking out the light ahead.

The light! A soft grey circle (mostly obscured by Bogsy) had appeared.

And I saw something else, as well: he'd got the wings. He must have brought them earlier – perhaps when he'd come out of school before everyone else – and hidden them at this end of the pipe. Now he was trying to get them (and himself) out again, but there was almost no room to move.

The man who's come out of the pub to check on his friend
shakes his head in surprise and looks up the road, then
back towards town. Back towards town, a tall figure is
running.

　'Titch! What's up? Where you going?'

　'Get my car!'

　'You can't, Titch! You've had too many!'

　The tall figure raises an arm as it runs, waving away
the objection – or waving goodbye. His friend, standing
watching him go, under the sign of The Bricklayer's
Arms, can't tell which.

The end of the pipe, when it came, was unexpected. The
light couldn't have been as distant as I'd thought. When
we emerged, the sun had nearly gone and the sky was
sombre. We crawled out into a rubbish tip, or perhaps just
some stuff thrown out by passing cars. There were take-
away boxes with gunk in, and bottles and, weirdly, a pair
of trousers. A fox must have been here, too: I put my hand
on something slimy, with bones and feathers.

'Eurghh!' It was half a dead pigeon. The stink brought my stomach up into my throat.

Bogsy paid no attention. He was squatting on his haunches, inspecting the wings. With his knees sticking out on either side, he looked more like a frog than a bird! But no one could see us, down there in the ditch.

Anyway, all the spectators, I guessed, must be well behind us now. The drain had led us past them, to the foot of the embankment.

I saw it all. From here, we would climb the embankment and get to the bridge. He'd planned it well: one of the trees growing up the embankment was rooted in the ditch itself, which meant we'd be able to move from ditch to slope without being seen. And we'd climb the slope, concealed by the trees, and be on the bridge itself before anyone knew anything about it.

PC Horn would be wondering why he'd listened to Peter's story. It was a hoax and a waste of time. A fairy tale. He'd start telling everyone to go home.

And then we'd appear.

Too late to be stopped.

Too late to get back-up.

Poor PC Horn.

And poor me. What chance did *either* of us have?

I watched Bogsy going over the wings with his fingers, smoothing the feathers, feeling the structure underneath.

Could I be the feather that wouldn't lie straight? I'd have to act fast.

When he was satisfied there was no damage, he grunted and said (though without looking up), 'Give us a hand with these.' It was the first time he'd spoken since leaving Lark Lane.

He gave me one of the wings to hold. I gripped it by its top edge. My heart was pounding. This was my moment.

'*Careful!*' said Bogsy because I was crushing the feathers.

He got to his feet, but crouching. I got to mine, but stood up straight.

'*Get down!*'

I opened my mouth to shout, *Over here!* They'd all come running and PC Horn would apprehend Bogsy.

I closed my mouth again and dropped down beside

him obediently. It wouldn't solve anything, calling for help. He'd only do it again later on, or do something else.

Something big had to happen. Here. Tonight.

And I had to let it. But also stop it. It didn't make sense.

Don't think too hard.

The car is trying to manoeuvre away from where it has parked, on the side of the Burstead Road. It touches the car in front, then reverses and bumps the one behind. How is it going to get anywhere, if it can't get out of its space?

Backwards and forwards it goes, getting more and more frantic, hitting the cars in front and behind. But slowly, slowly, its angle is changing.

Getting up the slope was worse than crawling through the drain. Far worse. It was dark in amongst the fir trees because they'd been planted so close together. (That would be to stop people doing exactly what we were doing.) There certainly weren't any paths, and the trees' lower branches were so near the ground, there wasn't even space to stand up. Not that standing up would have helped: the slope was so steep we were scrambling at best, bracing our feet against roots so we didn't slip back. I screwed up my eyes to protect them, and tried not to yell when a branch whipped my face or cut into my hand.

And somehow we pulled the wings behind us. They'd surely be damaged by *this*. Bogsy would have to accept that the feathers were going to look a mess now.

It seemed he did. What he minded about was the harness. Whenever it caught on a branch he said, '*Stop!*' and we had to wait, while he freed it, with painstaking care.

But at last we reached the top of the slope and came out from the horrible trees. They were still a screen between us and the people we'd left behind, down below. But ahead, the motorway roared and the sky opened out. Most of the daylight had gone from it now, but after the gloomy dark of the wood, it was still a relief.

The wings didn't look too bad, after all, and Bogsy was too excited to inspect them anyway this time. At least, I think that's what it was. He was constantly flexing his fingers and working the muscles in his jaw. It was weird. It was like he was back in his shed, right back at the start, chewing gum and positioning feathers. But he'd come too far to go back. In the narrow strip of verge between the trees and the rushing cars, I helped him on with his wings at last.

What else could I do? Maisie had said, *Trust your instincts.* Well, I was ready and waiting to trust them, but they were keeping themselves to themselves.

We had to climb over a barrier and haul ourselves up to a concrete ledge before we could set foot on the parapet of the bridge. And at this point, the bridge rested on the embankment, which meant two things. One: we were still concealed from spectators. Two: if we'd fallen, we'd only have fallen back into the trees. But, perhaps in preparation for what was to come, we flattened our chests and faces against the steel mesh bolted on to the railings. The parapet was so thin, our heels would have hung out over the edge if we hadn't turned our feet to the side like figures painted on Ancient Egyptian tombs. Bogsy could have been that bird god, if he hadn't thrown his mask away.

Like that, we edged along, gripping the railings and the mesh. What if a car going over the bridge was to spot us? But no, they all had their lights on; they wouldn't see anything but the road. If somebody glimpsed a boy with wings, they would think they were dreaming, and stop for a nap.

The wings hampered Bogsy. They didn't behave as they had in the shed, or even as they had when he'd worn them outside on Halloween night. The wind blew them every which way. And, now and then, it whipped them about so wildly they seemed to have a life of their own. He tried to control them by catching them in his fingers, but he couldn't do much.

And now the embankment was dropping away beneath us. The bridge reached out into empty air.

'Get to the middle!' yelled Bogsy. He had to raise his voice above the motorway noise.

The people below would see us now, too. Perhaps they would shout. If they did, there was no way we'd hear them. Only a giant's voice would reach us now. But we couldn't afford to look down, so we had no idea if they were trying. We couldn't afford to look down because now there'd be nothing beneath, except the drop, and we couldn't risk letting ourselves see that.

I never knew fear could feel like it did up there on the bridge. If you think you're going to die, people say, your whole life flashes before you. Well, that's not true. Or perhaps I wasn't at that stage. Because mine did the opposite. My past and my future *cut out*. What we were doing; why we were here; all that went. The only thing that mattered to me was the present. The present moment. My fingers, clutching the mesh; my Egyptian-style feet.

And I couldn't think what I should do, beyond carrying on. Hand over hand, shuffle shuffle. Don't stop. Don't stumble. Keep going. At least you're alive. I would have kept going for ever, I think, if something hadn't changed.

My feet felt it first. They no longer had to press in so tight to avoid jutting over the edge. Then my hands felt the railings begin to curve.

The parapet was widening! I looked, and saw we had entered a kind of small concrete bay.

It was there, perhaps, for maintenance workers: a place

of safety where they could unpack their tools. Whatever, it seemed we had actually reached the middle of the bridge. The bay wasn't spacious, but compared to the ledge that had brought us there, it was Wembley arena! The railings curved inwards, around it. We pressed ourselves into the curve and dared to face out and look down. On the crowd. If they were still there.

Far below us, they were. They stood still, looking up. Their faces were lit now and then by the lights of cars on Hinton Road. I couldn't make out individuals, only Peter Horn's dad, because he was taller. He seemed to have raised his hands. He was probably shouting.

I wanted to laugh. We were safe! We'd survived! It was like the time in the shed when we'd managed to leave Alan Tydman behind. We'd shaken him off, left him not knowing which way to turn. Only this was better.

It was more than better. In all the relief, I didn't look beyond it. So when Bogsy yelled, 'Ready?' I couldn't think what he meant.

'For what?' I joked. 'Tea?' I could say what I liked, there was no way he'd hear.

But Bogsy was yelling again. 'Come on, *stupid*! Put your hand on my back!'

I couldn't think why he wanted me to. But then . . .

Don't think.

The sun had set.

He was going too fast.

Stepping forward towards the edge.

'*Push* when I say!' he screamed – and almost immediately after: '*NOW!*'

And he jumped.

SMACK!

That's the sound of a car being driven into the ditch. Normally, people will stare at a crash, but the people standing on Hinton Road carry on looking up. The sun is about to set. No one can tear their eyes away from the bridge. Not even the big bully boy, who tried for a while to appear unconcerned. Not even the policeman.

The man called Titch (whose real name is Colin) climbs out of his car and staggers towards them. He looks where they're looking.

The sun is about to set and, against the darkening sky, two figures are silhouetted. He recognizes one, even at this distance, straight away. It seems to have wings.

His wife didn't mention wings. He's definitely had a few too many. Then again, his wife didn't go into that much detail. 'Get to the bridge!' she screamed down the phone. 'For God's sake! Be quick! If you won't, I will . . .'

But he is too late.

The sun has set.

Up on the bridge, against the sky, the figure with wings has stepped forward and spread them.

The man on the ground holds his head in his hands and groans. He falls to his knees.

And the winged figure jumps.

CHAPTER 27
THE FALL OF ICARUS

What did he think, as he fell? As he tumbled out of the sky, trailing feathers?

How much time did he have? Could he think at all?

Did his whole life flash before him, as it should?

And, if so, did he ask,

Was it worth it?

Was what worth it?

The glory of flight.

This was his thought:

Was the glory worthwhile?

Well, was it?

Worth what?

Dying for.

That was his thought

(And his answer?)

as he fell

towards

the sea.

CHAPTER 28

MEADOWS AND MARSH

'NO!'

That was me.

When Bogsy told me to put my hand on his back, I felt the strap I had helped him to test just a few days before. I hadn't expected to feel it, but instinct said grab it, so I did.

I didn't push, I pulled.

And when he jumped, I couldn't have held him, except that the fingers of my other hand had locked on to the mesh at my back.

He threw himself forward in the harness, as I had done in the shed that time; as I'd seen a falcon do once, at a fair, when a man had it tied to his hand, and it tried to fly.

Then he collapsed on the concrete, with me still holding

on to the strap. I thought he'd fainted, but he hadn't. He grabbed my leg. He'd not given up.

And so we fought.

'Mate! Mate!' The policeman is shaking the newcomer by the shoulders. 'Mate! D'you know him? He hasn't gone!'

We fought as we had in the shed, down amongst the chewing gum wrappers and old apple cores. We fought like that. Only that was for fun. This was high up, on a ledge, with nothing to stop us falling off. We weren't trying to make each other eat orange peel now. We were fighting for Bogsy's life. The concrete was cruelly hard. It grazed our elbows and near cracked our skulls, but that was nothing. In our ears, the motorway roared for blood.

The man on his knees looks up, first at the policeman, then at the bridge. What's happening up there? The two figures have gone. But no, they haven't – they're rolling around together on the narrow platform. The man groans again when the struggle brings them close to the edge.

'His dad!' he says, though he can't tell which is which any more. He begins to sob. 'I'm his useless dad!'

And it could have gone either way. We were equally matched – that is, equally bad. The only thing was, he was wearing the wings, which made it easier for me to pin him down. But, then again, we could have *both* gone over.

The policeman shakes the other man again. 'Pull yourself together!' And as he speaks, the crowd gasps and parts because something is falling towards them. Tumbling out of the sky, trailing feathers, it crashes on to the road.

Not a boy, but a wing.

And it's followed by something else, smaller, which lands close by and unnerves them because it's so ordinary-looking.

At one point, with a tearing sound, one wing got ripped right off. I flung it aside and it must have fallen down to the crowd below. Soon after, I lost a shoe, which went the same way. Signals, from us to them, that the Icarus Show was no longer as advertised. If they'd bought tickets, they could have complained. But they hadn't. The show was free.

'Make contact!' says the policeman urgently. He's trying not to shout. 'Let him know it's you. Tell him something he needs to hear.'

But the man can think of nothing.

'Come on!' The policeman is losing it now, despite all his training. 'Come on, man! Tell him he's going to be OK!'

The cold wind blows through the bridge and the black night wraps everything in despair.

The man is shrinking into himself. He's giving up.

But no, he's gathering himself. He's getting up.

And now he towers over everyone else. He's filling his great lungs with cold night air.

And his voice is the voice of a giant, powerful enough to make itself heard over any distance, over all other noise.

'DAVEY!'

Bogsy went limp. To be on the safe side, I sat on his chest, but I knew it wasn't a trick.

The voice wasn't PC Horn's. *He* hadn't been able to make himself heard. Someone else must have come. And when I looked cautiously down, I understood.

I was right, someone else *had* arrived. And I knew who he was straight away, by his height. The last time I'd seen him, he'd been holding a stack of boxes in his arms. He'd been big and strong enough to carry a TV, a microwave and a load of books, all at the same time.

Sitting on Bogsy's chest, I relaxed. I may even have patted his shoulder.

They got us down with one of those cranes they use to fix street lamps and clean office windows. It had an extending arm with a pod on the end. The pod contained PC Horn, who helped us climb in. Everyone clapped when we reached the ground.

Bogsy went straight to his dad, who gave him a bear hug, wrapping him up completely, for two or three seconds, in his great big coat. Another happy ending.

Then Colin Marsh faced the crowd and said, 'Thanks, everyone.' Even though they'd done nothing but turn up to watch. He was thanking Alan Tydman and Rob and Jack, which seemed ironic. He wouldn't have done if he'd known. But perhaps he only meant thanks for clapping. That must have been it.

Cars kept going past, with their headlights on, and in one of these moments, I caught sight of Alan. He was staring at Bogsy in total amazement. His mouth was open. Perhaps he was just surprised by Bogsy's face, but I think it was more than that. Things were changing.

'Thanks,' said Colin Marsh to Peter Horn's dad, and PC Horn said, 'Don't thank me, mate. Thank *him*.'

I was standing alone, by the crane. Colin Marsh came over and shook my hand. *His* hand was huge, and while mine was in it, it felt warm and safe.

He said, 'I owe you one,' and I said, 'S'OK.'

Then PC Horn was shouting something about sorting out a car. Colin Marsh went back and they all moved off down the road. I didn't go with them. There seemed to be a car in the ditch. In all the excitement, they left me behind.

Our two bikes were just where we'd left them, a little apart from everyone else's. I guessed he'd come back tomorrow for his. Right now, he wouldn't be thinking about it. He wouldn't want to bother with unimportant things. Or people. There'd be lots, I guessed, from the past few weeks that wouldn't matter to him now.

Just before I set off, I lifted my hands from the handlebars one at a time, to blow on them briefly. I knew they'd only stay warm for a second, but I did it, all the same.

And that's when I heard the footsteps. Someone was running up the road. Not fast – almost stumbling – but nonetheless running, *pit-pat* on the tarmac. Louder and louder, coming towards me.

'Oi, wait!' called a voice.

It was him.

He'd slipped away from the rest, and come back.

In the headlights of a passing car I saw that, although his face was still bad, both eyes were open again. He was panting so much that at first, when he reached me, it was hard for him to speak. He bent over with his hands on his knees, elbows out, and, from that position, said, 'Thanks.' More panting. 'Thanks, OK? For getting my dad.'

I didn't, I wanted to say. Him thinking I had was like when he'd thought I'd been clever enough to work Icarus out. I knew it was no good pretending any more. I'd never be clever enough for him. I swallowed.

'It was Maisie,' I said. Because suddenly that's who I realized it had to have been.

I waited for him to say *Oh* and go back to his dad. Up on the bridge, he had called me stupid.

But he just said, 'Well, anyway. Thanks.' He didn't seem to mind.

'She must have phoned your mum,' I went on.

And suddenly he laughed. 'She'd know the number: we never changed it!'

Maisie had not only shown me how to save Bogsy, she'd saved the day, too.

I caught his mood and laughed myself. I put on a posh accent. 'Jolly good show!'

I hoped he'd pick up on it, call me 'old chap' or something. But he didn't. With Bogsy, you never quite knew where you were.

Then I had an idea and tried something else. In my normal voice, I said, 'Happy birthday!'

There'd be hours and hours of trouble ahead, for sure. Talking and trouble, for him and for me. Meadows and Marsh: it sounded like part of the landscape. But for now, we didn't need to think about that.

He didn't pick up on the Happy Birthday, though. He looked quickly over his shoulder to check his dad was still off by the car. Then he picked up his bike. 'C'mon. Let's go.'

He didn't say where. Home, probably, but you never knew, with him. It was exciting.

Neither of us had lights, it turned out, which was a dangerous thing. You could be stopped by a policeman for that, but PC Horn was down in the ditch and didn't even notice.

After all – I mean, after the things that had happened that night, and compared to the ones that might happen tomorrow, next week, next year – it didn't really matter.

CHAPTER 29
GUESS WHO

Hey. My turn now. Me.

Not him any more.

He's all right, but he gets things wrong. I been reading this. He's not gonna mess up the ending.

And he's got *that* wrong. This *isn't* the ending. Not if you ask me.

But he did get some things right.

Or I wouldn't be here.

And something *she* was right about. It's good to work with someone. Better than working on your own. Yeah, me saying that.

But you got to have ambition.

I'm gonna paint the Mona Lisa. He can watch.

He makes it sound too cosy. Wants it to be like his railway book. It's not. He thinks I'm gonna go back to building walls. But that was then.

You can't go through what I been through –

You can't go through what I been through and not change.

I might rebuild his old shed. Or I might knock it down. With his old cat inside. Not so cosy, see?

I might even –

I'm gonna build the Eiffel Tower.

He's all right. And I got ambition, enough for us both. We'll be OK.

Time to hit the road.

Hey, world, you ready?

I got plans.

PS Only joking about the cat.